THE MIDNIGHT ORDER

by Jace Garth

Second edition 2024

ISBN: 978-0-646-89121-7

*To my beautiful wife Anna-Liese
and all of our children*

The Midnight Order

by Jace Garth

CHAPTER 1.1: A SKEPTIC'S PURSUIT

Tim gazed out the window of his home office, his eyes fixated on the distant outline of the skyline, obscured by a gentle morning haze. Mernda, the suburban sanctuary he called home, was comfortably nestled on the outer-northern edge of the city of Melbourne, providing a calm refuge for his restless mind.

In his mid-20s, Tim's boyish face still held onto an innocence that belied his sharp intellect and relentless pursuit of facts. As an investigative journalist, he had cut his teeth on exposing corruption and deceit, unmasking the façade that often shrouded reality. He was a seeker of knowledge, a man driven by logical explanations and empirical evidence. To him, the inexplicable had to be explicable.

His eyes drifted to his reflection in the window of his three-storey townhouse. The shadows seemed to dance behind him, and for a brief moment, he saw a glimmer, a fleeting glimpse of something in the corner of his eye. He turned sharply, his heart skipping a beat, but found nothing amiss. An involuntary shudder ran down his spine as he remembered other instances where objects seemed to move of their own accord, or when he thought he caught sight of one of his deceased pets.

These occurrences he dismissed as figments of his imagination, a mind playing tricks due to stress or fatigue. He refused to give credence to anything beyond the physical world, denying the supernatural its foothold in his beliefs. The world was governed by laws and rules, and there had to be an explanation for everything.

A chime from his computer broke his reverie, and he found an email from a colleague in his inbox. Attached was an article detailing strange happenings in the city of Melbourne. Residents reported unexplainable phenomena: shadows moving without source, sudden chills, whispers in the wind.

Tim's eyes narrowed as he read the accounts. These stories had the trappings of urban myths, the kind that would spread like wildfire through a small community. It was precisely the sort of thing that caught the public's imagination, and something that he could debunk with careful investigation.

A smirk spread across his face. He began to type, his fingers flying across the keyboard, responding to his colleague's email. "I'm on it," he wrote. "Expect a sensational piece tearing down these bizarre tales."

He looked up local contacts in the city of Melbourne, finding a town hall official and a couple of residents who had witnessed the strange events. Tim knew that the key to a good story was firsthand accounts, and he wanted to be the one to unearth the truth behind the sensationalism.

As he prepared to embark on his journey to the city, Tim couldn't shake off a nagging feeling that something was drawing him towards this investigation. Was it merely the challenge of debunking the myths, or was there something deeper, something hidden that yearned to be uncovered?

CHAPTER 1.2: THE ROAD TO MELBOURNE

Tim's home office had become a nexus of information and preparation. Spread across his desk were historical records, maps, and transcripts of interviews with Melbourne's residents. His computer screen was filled with tabs and documents, each detailing a different aspect of the city's oddities.

The past held peculiarities for Melbourne. In the late 1800s, there were reports of sudden temperature drops that lasted only moments, unexplained sounds echoing across the city, and even sightings of apparitions in the city's laneways on foggy nights. More recently, residents spoke of a chilling wind that seemed to follow them, shadows that behaved oddly, and voices carried by the breeze.

Tim found himself fascinated by the anecdotes and the way they were woven into the fabric of the city's identity. Yet, as an investigative journalist, he knew that sensationalism could easily distort facts. He was determined to approach the matter scientifically, armed with reason and logic.

His equipment was spread out on the floor, ready to be packed. A professional-grade camera with various lenses, a digital voice recorder, infrared thermometers, and an anemometer to measure wind speed. He also packed a notebook, filled with his research notes, contacts in the city, and a checklist of phenomena he intended to investigate. He wasn't hunting for ghosts; he was searching for explanations.

As Tim loaded his gear into his car, he couldn't help but reflect on his past investigations. He had exposed corruption within powerful corporations, unveiled fraud in political campaigns, and brought to light hidden injustices. In each case, he had been driven by the desire to find facts hidden beneath layers of deceit.

But Melbourne's city was different. This was a place veiled in folklore and community tales, not lies or corruption. The challenge was to separate reality from exaggeration, to find the mundane explanations behind what seemed otherworldly.

The drive to the centre of Melbourne was a journey from almost remote to a bustling city. As Tim navigated the roads, the occasional grassy paddock and sprawling countryside of the naturally beautiful Australian landscape gave way to increasingly taller buildings and busier streets. The contrast was striking, and Tim found himself increasingly curious at to what lied in store for him.

He put on some music, letting the rhythm soothe his mind as the streets rolled by. His thoughts drifted back to his own strange experiences. How could he so easily dismiss what he had seen or felt when he was about to challenge a city's belief in the supernatural?

As the kilometres ticked away, Tim considered his skepticism. It was a shield, a defence against the unknown. He had always found comfort in evidence and facts, in knowing that there was a logical explanation for everything. But was he being too rigid? Was there room for questions that didn't have easy answers?

His mind wandered to his childhood, to the teachings of his school teachers and the wisdom of his parents. They had instilled in him the importance of inquiry, the value of asking questions, and the courage to challenge assumptions.

But Melbourne was a place of living history, where stories were passed down through generations, where the unknown was embraced rather than feared.

Tim's grip tightened on the steering wheel as the signs for the city of Melbourne showed his imminent arrival. The city was now a tangible destination, no longer an abstract concept hidden in records and interviews. His heartbeat quickened, anticipation mingling with a hint of trepidation.

As he entered the city, the world seemed to shift slightly, as if acknowledging his arrival. The streets were busy, the tall buildings holding the watchful gaze of a community aware of its reputation.

Tim parked his car and took a deep breath. The adventure had begun, and he was in the heart of the mystery. His logical mind told him that he was here to debunk myths, to bring reason to the irrational. But a small voice within whispered that he was here to discover, to learn, and perhaps, to challenge his own beliefs.

The road to Melbourne's city had brought him to the threshold of the unknown. Now it was time to step through, armed with curiosity and guided by skepticism, ready to unravel the secrets that lay hidden in the shadows of this otherwise internationally-renowned city.

CHAPTER 1.3: GATHERING IN MELBOURNE

Tim's day in the bustling city of Melbourne began with an urgency that matched the fast pace of the streets. The towering buildings, the sound of trams, and the chatter of pedestrians filled the air with a symphony of urban life. But beneath the surface, Tim could sense something more, an undercurrent of intrigue that seemed to cling to the very essence of the city.

His first task was to gather his team. The chosen ones for this mission were not seasoned investigators, but people he trusted and knew well. Each had a unique perspective that would contribute to uncovering the reality behind the strange occurrences in Melbourne.

First was Georgia, Tim's younger sister. Her bright eyes and playful "Princess-style" demeanour were a contrast to the seriousness of the task at hand. Yet, her friendly nature had a way of drawing people in, a trait that would prove useful in talking to the city's residents.

Then there was Noah, Georgia's friend and flatmate. Quiet and shy, he often stayed in the background, but his intelligence was evident in his thoughtful gaze. He was the logical thinker, the analyser, someone who would question every detail and help to see past superficial explanations.

Finally, Heidi, Tim's work colleague, joined the group. She was friendly but a realist. Her eyes sparkled with the determination to get to the point, to understand how things worked. She was the anchor, the voice of reason that would keep the team focused.

As they gathered in Federation Square, the vibrant public space in the heart of Melbourne, Tim briefed them on the task. They were to investigate the reports of strange phenomena, to explore the city's history, and to talk to residents to get their perspective.

They each had their opinions about the occurrences. Georgia was open-minded, excited by the possibilities, while Noah approached it with skepticism, eager to find a logical explanation. Heidi's attitude was pragmatic; as a journalist, she wanted facts, not folklore.

Their first stop was the State Library of Victoria, an iconic building that held the city's historical records. Tim and his team spent hours pouring over old newspapers, maps, and photographs. The past was a treasure trove of information, hinting at events that seemed unexplainable but were most likely products of the time and the imagination of the people.

Leaving the library, they ventured into the busy streets, guided by Tim's research and intuition. They talked to shopkeepers, cafe owners, and pedestrians, asking about their experiences and their thoughts on the strange occurrences.

The reactions were mixed. Some laughed off the questions, dismissing them as mere urban legends. Others were more thoughtful, sharing personal stories or directing them to someone who might know more. A few seemed uneasy, their eyes darting as if they were afraid to speak, as if the city itself was listening.

The day wore on, and the city's pulse began to slow as evening approached. The team gathered at a local cafe to discuss their findings. Tim listened as Georgia shared anecdotes with excitement, as Noah dissected the logic behind the stories, and while Heidi summarised the facts.

They were a cohesive unit, their differences complementing each other, their common goal driving them forward. Yet, the city remained an enigma, its secrets veiled by the daily life of its residents.

As night fell, Melbourne transformed. The shadows grew longer, the streets quieter, and the lights of the skyscrapers cast a glow that seemed to add to the city's mystique. Tim stood at a street corner, looking up at the night sky framed by towering structures, and felt a shiver run down his spine.

The city was alive, its heartbeat echoing in the silence, its soul whispering in the wind. It was a place of contradictions, of beauty and complexity, of logic and emotion. It held its history close, guarding its secrets with a quiet dignity.

Tim knew that their investigation had only just begun. Melbourne was not going to reveal itself easily. It would challenge them, test their resolve, and make them question their beliefs.

But he was ready. With Georgia's warmth, Noah's intellect, and Heidi's realism, they were a formidable team. Together, they would peel back the layers of the city, explore its hidden corners, and seek the answers that lay beneath the surface.

For Melbourne was not just a city; it was a puzzle, a riddle waiting to be solved. And Tim and his team were determined to unravel it, to understand its essence, and to find the reality behind the myths.

The city awaited them, its stories ready to be told, its mysteries ready to be uncovered. It was a journey into the unknown, guided by passion, reason, and a desire to discover.

The adventure had only just begun.

CHAPTER 1.4: WHISPERS AT THE QUARTER

Nestled in bustling Degraves Street in Melbourne's CBD, The Quarter was an eclectic blend of old-world charm and contemporary flair. The rough wooden floors, cushioned wall panels, and modern art pieces created an ambience both cosy and chic. It was the perfect place for Tim and his companions to unwind after a day of investigations.

Tim was the first to arrive, securing a table near the window that overlooked the busy street. The murmur of conversation and the clatter of dishes filled the air as he scanned the menu. Shortly after, Georgia arrived, her face lit with excitement.

"Tim!" she called, rushing over to hug her brother. "I can't wait to hear about what you've found!"

Tim smiled, greeting her warmly. "Patience, Georgia. Noah and Heidi are on their way."

Soon, the four were seated, menus closed, and glasses filled.

"So," Georgia began, her eyes sparkling, "What's the latest? Any haunted houses or spooky shadows?"

Tim chuckled, "It's not about ghosts, Georgia. It's about the unexplained, the hidden corners of reality."

Noah added quietly, "There's more to the world than meets the eye. You've seen it yourself, Tim."

Heidi raised an eyebrow. "But let's be clear, we're here to investigate facts, not chase fairytales."

Their conversation flowed, touching on rumours, skepticism, beliefs, and the thrill of the unknown. Tim led them through his findings, maintaining his scientific approach, while the others offered their perspectives.

Elizabeth, a young barista, couldn't help but overhear their conversation as she moved between tables. Her eyes widened as she listened, curiosity growing. Finally, she approached their table.

"Excuse me," she said, her voice soft yet firm. "I couldn't help but overhear your conversation. You're talking about the strange events around the city, aren't you?"

The group turned, surprised but not displeased by the interruption.

"That's right," Tim replied, studying her. "Do you know something about it?"

Elizabeth hesitated, then leaned closer. "Just be careful," she whispered. "Some things are better left alone."

The warning hung in the air as she moved away, leaving the four to ponder her words.

Their dinner continued, the conversation turning to lighter topics. Yet, Tim's mind remained on Elizabeth's words. As they prepared to leave, he noticed something odd —a flicker of shadow, a subtle shift in the reflection of the window. He turned, but saw nothing unusual.

The night ended with laughter and farewells, but as Tim walked back to his car, he couldn't shake the feeling that something significant had begun. The subtle movement in the reflection of the restaurant's window lingered in his mind, foreshadowing the mystery to come.

A chill ran down his spine, but he shrugged it off, attributing it to the cool

Melbourne air. But deep down, he knew something more was at play.

CHAPTER 2.1: VOICES OF MELBOURNE

Now settled in the heart of Melbourne, Tim embarked on the first phase of his investigation. The city was a thriving metropolis filled with people from all walks of life, and Tim knew that the key to understanding the mysterious occurrences lay in the collective memories and experiences of the locals.

His first stop was a vintage bookstore, owned by an elderly gentleman named Mr. Archer Cooper. The narrow aisles were lined with shelves packed with books, each one a silent witness to the history and secrets of Melbourne.

"Strange occurrences?" Archer repeated Tim's question, stroking his thin beard. "Ah, yes, many people have reported seeing unusual things. But you know how it is, young man. Imagination often gets the best of people."

He dismissed the idea with a wave of his hand, but Tim could see a flicker of uncertainty in his eyes. He thanked Archer.

Tim and made a note in his journal. He was careful to document everything, from body language to the exact words used, building a comprehensive picture.

Next, he spoke with a local historian, Dr. Wilson, who was more than eager to share her extensive knowledge.

"The city has always had its share of myths and legends," she told Tim, her voice filled with passion. "From spectral apparitions to unexplained sounds, Melbourne has a rich tapestry of stories. But are they real? Who's to say? History often blurs the line between fact and fiction."

Tim listened intently, jotting down her insights, appreciating her academic perspective. She provided him with several historical references, pointing him in directions that might further his research.

A visit to a busy market led him to a young shopkeeper, Sarah, who was less eager to talk. Her eyes widened as Tim mentioned his investigation, and she glanced nervously over her shoulder.

"You should be careful, sir," she whispered, leaning closer. "Some say there are forces at work here that no one understands. People have seen things, heard things. It's best not to meddle."

Tim assured her that he was taking a rational approach, but her words struck a chord. The fear in her eyes was genuine, and he couldn't help but wonder what had caused it.

As the days turned into weeks, Tim's investigation took him to various corners of Melbourne, from busy streets to quiet parks. He spoke to teachers, artists, police officers, and even tourists, each providing a unique perspective. Some were dismissive, laughing off the strange occurrences as mere superstitions. Others were more contemplative, sharing personal experiences that were both puzzling and intriguing.

Throughout it all, Tim maintained his skepticism. He was a man of science, not superstition, and he knew that the truth often lay hidden beneath layers of fear and misunderstanding. Yet, the more he delved into the stories and experiences of the townsfolk, the more he felt a nagging sense of unease.

There was a pattern emerging, subtle connections that hinted at something more profound. Each story was a piece of a puzzle, and Tim knew that putting them together would lead him to something significant.

He returned to his temporary apartment each night, poring over his notes, piecing together the information. He felt the pull of the unknown, the thrill of the chase. But he was also aware of a growing sensation, a feeling that he was being watched, that something was lurking just out of sight.

He brushed it off as the product of his intense focus on the subject, reminding himself that he was here to seek answers, not to succumb to irrational fears.

But as he closed his journal and turned off the light, he couldn't shake the thought that the city of Melbourne, with its boutique shops and hidden laneways, was holding onto a secret. A secret that was waiting to be uncovered, a riddle that begged to be solved.

And Tim knew that he was the one who had to unravel it.

CHAPTER 2.2: SHADOWS OF THE PAST

Tim's investigation was beginning to bear fruit, but the more he uncovered, the more complex the puzzle became. He found himself standing at the precipice of a vast well of history, with tendrils that reached back generations. It was time to call in reinforcements, and Heidi, with her sharp analytical skills, was the perfect partner.

He invited her into his lounge room, which he had turned into a makeshift research centre. Walls were plastered with photographs, maps, newspaper clippings, and handwritten notes. Tables were strewn with books, historical records, and personal anecdotes.

"Quite the setup you have here," Heidi remarked, her eyes wide as she surveyed the room.

"It's a big project," Tim replied with a small smile. "I need all the help I can get. Georgia and Noah are busy with school assignments."

Heidi's presence was a welcome addition. She brought a fresh perspective and a knack for connecting the dots. Together, they delved into Melbourne's archives, poring over old newspapers and historical documents, searching for clues to the unexplained events.

A pattern soon emerged. The strange occurrences seemed to centre around a well-known historical landmark – the platforms and upstairs ballroom at Flinders Street Station. Reports of unusual phenomena dated back over a century, each event unique but tied to the same locale.

"What do you make of this, Tim?" Heidi asked, holding up a faded newspaper clipping from 1927. "It describes a confused-looking man holding a fishing rod that would walk towards the riverbank before vanishing without a trace."

"It's consistent with other reports," Tim said thoughtfully. "Apparitions, visual distortions, unaccountable noises. They all seem to occur around the station."

Heidi's journalistic instincts were stirred by the mystery, but she remained focused on finding rational explanations. "There must be a logical reason," she insisted. "Perhaps geological anomalies, or some kind of atmospheric condition unique to that area," even though she was starting to think those explanations were not going to close out the mystery.

Tim nodded, appreciating her grounded approach. "We need to keep digging. The answers are here; we just have to find them."

Days turned into weeks as they immersed themselves in the past, uncovering accounts from local residents, some of whom had witnessed the phenomena firsthand. One elderly woman recounted a tale of a ghostly figure seen walking near the tower late at night. A librarian shared a story of a mysterious hum that seemed to emanate from the tower's walls.

They managed to track down a retired police officer who had been called to Flinders Street Station one stormy night in 1973. He had found the doors to the upper ballroom inexplicably wide open, lights flickering, yet no one was inside.

"I've never forgotten that night," he told them, his voice still tinged with disbelief. "I saw a lot in my career, but nothing like that. It felt... unnatural."

Tim and Heidi were meticulous in their research, refusing to let emotion or speculation cloud their judgement. Yet the more they discovered, the more the intrigue deepened.

They visited Flinders Street Station several times, walking its ancient train platforms, feeling the weight of history in the worn stairs. Tim couldn't shake the feeling that the ancient building was hiding something, a secret locked away in its shadows.

As they stood beneath the towering structure, Heidi turned to Tim, her eyes filled with determination. "We need to understand what's happening here, Tim. Not just for the story, but for ourselves."

"I agree," Tim said, his gaze fixed on the station's famous façade. "There's something here, something that defies explanation. But we'll find the answer. We have to."

They continued to dig, reaching further back in time, uncovering incidents that predated the building itself. The land upon which it was built seemed to be the common thread, a place imbued with an inexplicable energy.

And then, a breakthrough.

An old journal, tucked away in the corner of a dusty library, contained the personal notes of a 19th-century scientist. He had conducted extensive studies on the land, documenting strange magnetic anomalies and unexplained fluctuations in the Earth's electromagnetic field.

The journal provided new avenues of exploration, connecting pieces of the puzzle that had long remained disjointed. Tim and Heidi's excitement grew as they realised they were on the brink of something extraordinary.

Yet, even as the pieces began to fall into place, Tim couldn't shake a growing sense of unease. Flinders Street Station, with its hidden secrets, loomed large in his thoughts. Its shadows seemed to stretch beyond the physical world, reaching into the very fabric of existence.

The city of Melbourne had a dark and hidden history, a tapestry woven with threads of the unexplained. And as Tim and Heidi delved deeper, they found themselves drawn into a mystery that transcended time and reason.

A mystery that beckoned, whispered in the wind, and called to them from the shadows of the past. A mystery that refused to be silenced.

CHAPTER 2.3: ECHOES OF THE UNSEEN

Tim had always been a man of logic, a seeker of explanations grounded in science and reason. But as the investigation unfolded, the things he began to experience defied his rational mind. Objects in his house seemed to move of their own accord, shadows shifted in the corners of his eyes, and disembodied sounds whispered through the silence of the night.

It started subtly. One morning, he found his research papers scattered across the floor, though he had left them neatly stacked on the table the night before. He attributed it to a gust of wind from an open window, but a lingering doubt gnawed at his mind.

The occurrences escalated. A cup of coffee slid across the table without a touch. A door slammed shut with no one near it. Tim's recording equipment, left on to document his findings, captured inexplicable phenomena: a faint hum in the air, a sudden drop in temperature, a shadow passing by with no source.

His skepticism wavered. These were not mere coincidences or tricks of the mind. These were tangible events, captured on tape, witnessed with his own eyes.

He reached out to Georgia, Noah, and Heidi, seeking their insights. Had they seen anything? Experienced anything unusual? Their responses added further complexity to the unfolding mystery.

Georgia spoke of a feeling, a sense that she was being watched. She had heard footsteps behind her on a deserted street, turned to find no one there. A chill ran down her spine, a sensation that lingered long after the moment had passed.

Noah had encountered anomalies in his readings. Instruments malfunctioning without explanation, data that made no logical sense. He was intrigued, his analytical mind probing the puzzle from every angle.

Heidi, too, had seen things she couldn't explain. Lights flickering in her home, a reflection in the mirror that wasn't her own. She had felt a presence, an energy that pulsed through the very air.

Together, they gathered their findings, their observations, their fears, and their fascinations. Tim played the recordings, his hands trembling slightly as the eerie sounds filled the room.

"This can't be real," he whispered, his voice tinged with disbelief.

"It's real, Tim," Heidi said softly, her eyes filled with understanding. "We all know it. We've all felt it."

"What are we dealing with?" Georgia asked, her voice tight with anxiety. "What is happening to us?"

"We must remain objective," Noah cautioned, his scientific mind still seeking logic in the chaos. "We need more data, more evidence. We can't let fear cloud our judgement."

They agreed to continue their investigation, to delve deeper into the unknown, to seek answers in the face of the unexplainable.

Days turned into weeks, and the phenomena persisted. Tim's house became a focal point, a nexus of unexplained activity. He found himself waking in the night, feeling a presence in the room, hearing whispers that had no source.

He began to see things in the shadows, shapes that moved, eyes that watched. He captured more evidence on tape, visual distortions that danced across the screen, sounds that echoed with no origin.

His mind, once firmly grounded in reason, began to unravel. Doubt crept in, fear took hold, and the boundaries between reality and the inexplicable blurred.

"I don't know what's happening," he confessed, his eyes wide and haunted. "I can't explain it. I can't understand it."

Georgia reached out, her hand on his arm, her eyes filled with empathy. "We're in this together, Tim. We'll figure it out. We have to."

They poured over the evidence, the tapes, the photographs, the readings. They compared notes, shared experiences, sought patterns in the chaos.

And slowly, a picture began to emerge. The phenomena were not random; they were focused, directed. They seemed to be communicating, reaching out, calling to them.

Tim's house, once a place of comfort and refuge, became a conduit, a bridge between worlds. The more they delved into the mystery, the more the unseen forces reached out to them.

They felt it in the air, a vibration that resonated with their very souls. They saw it in the shadows, a movement that beckoned them closer. They heard it in the silence, a voice that whispered secrets in the dark.

The city of Melbourne, with its rich history and hidden secrets, had awakened something ancient, something powerful. Flinders Street Station, the epicentre of the phenomena, pulsed with an energy that transcended time and space.

The more they uncovered, the more they were drawn in, pulled toward an understanding that lay just beyond their grasp.

Tim, once a skeptic, now stood on the edge of belief, his mind open to possibilities he had never before considered. The evidence was there, the experiences were real, the phenomena were undeniable.

But what did it mean? What were they being called to discover? What lay at the heart of the mystery?

The answers eluded them, hidden in the shadows of the past, wrapped in layers of intrigue and complexity. But they knew they were close, that they were on the brink of something profound.

They were no longer mere observers; they were participants, connected to the unseen, part of a puzzle that spanned generations.

And as they stood at the threshold of the unknown, they knew that they were not alone, that they were being watched, guided, led.

They knew that the mystery was not just a story to be told but a journey to be taken.

A journey that had only just begun.

CHAPTER 2.4: UNRAVELLING REALITY

Tim had never been one to get rattled easily. As a seasoned journalist, he'd seen enough to have developed a thick skin and a rational mind. But what was about to transpire would challenge every foundation he'd built his beliefs upon.

Heidi, Georgia, Noah, and Tim were at Flinders Street Station, the landmark that had been at the centre of the unexplained events they had been investigating. The large clocks overlooking the bustling intersection were ticking away, witnesses to the countless stories that had unfolded at the heart of Melbourne.

The evening was drawing to a close. Shadows lengthened, and the golden light of the setting sun bathed the front of the station in a warm glow. Street musicians played their songs, and the murmur of the city filled the air.

Heidi was the first to notice something peculiar.

"Tim, look at that," she said, pointing towards a shadow that seemed to detach itself from a corner of the station and move along the wall.

Tim looked, squinting his eyes. "Probably just a trick of the light."

"No, I saw it too," Georgia chimed in, her voice tinged with excitement.

Tim's skeptical mind was at work, but his eyes couldn't deny what they were witnessing. A shadow, defying physics and logic, moving independent of any source. His heart raced, and he could feel the hairs on the back of his neck standing up.

They continued to watch, mesmerised, as the shadow danced its way along the wall, taking forms and shapes that seemed almost human. Then, just as suddenly as it had appeared, it vanished.

"That can't be real," Noah whispered, his voice betraying his disbelief.

But the unsettling event was not over. As Tim looked down at his notebook, he found the pages flipping by themselves, stopping at the detailed notes he'd taken about the landmark's history.

"What's going on?" Heidi demanded, her realistic approach giving way to genuine concern.

Tim couldn't answer. He was frozen, watching as his pen rolled across the table, pushed by an unseen force.

It was Georgia who finally broke the silence. "We can't ignore this, Tim. We've seen it with our own eyes."

Tim's mind was racing. This was not just a shadow on the wall or a breeze flipping the pages of a book. This was something more, something that defied all logical explanation.

The silence that had descended was broken by the distant tolling of the Flinders Street Station clock. Time seemed to have stopped, and the bustling city around them felt miles away.

Tim looked at his friends, their faces reflecting the confusion and fear he felt. "I don't know what this is," he admitted, his voice cracking. "But we have to find out."

As they left the station, Tim couldn't shake the feeling that something had fundamentally changed. The world, once so grounded and predictable, had revealed a crack, a flaw in its design. And he had been chosen to peer through it.

That night, Tim lay in bed, the events of the day replaying in his mind. He knew that he couldn't turn back, that he had crossed a line from which there was no return.

His rational mind fought to make sense of what he'd seen, but it was a losing battle. Something deep within him had been awakened, a realisation that the world was not as it seemed.

As sleep finally overtook him, he knew that he was on a path that would either lead to an extraordinary discovery or to the unravelling of his very sanity. The mystery of Flinders Street Station had become his obsession, and he would stop at nothing to uncover some answers to what were becoming some very peculiar questions.

CHAPTER 2.5: CONFRONTING THE UNSEEN

In the dimly lit living room of Tim's house, the group was gathered, each lost in thought, replaying the events at Flinders Street Station. The usual chatter and laughter were absent, replaced by an unsettling silence.

Tim, sitting on the couch with his hands clasped, was a picture of concentration. His mind was a whirlwind of conflicting emotions and thoughts. The journalist in him wanted facts, explanations, and logical conclusions. But the man in him could not deny what he had seen, what they had all witnessed.

Georgia, ever the optimist, was the first to break the silence. "We have to admit, Tim, that something truly strange is happening here."

Tim looked at her, his eyes narrowed, his brow furrowed. "Strange, yes. But there must be an explanation."

"You still think there's a rational explanation for all this?" Noah asked, his tone incredulous.

Tim sighed, running his fingers through his hair. "I want to believe there is. But I don't know anymore."

Heidi leaned forward. "Maybe it's time we accept that not everything can be explained by science or logic. Maybe there's more to this world than we can see or understand."

The words hung in the air, heavy with meaning and implication.

Tim looked at his group, each person showing a different emotion. Georgia seemed to glow with excitement, Noah's face wore an expression of confusion, and Heidi's eyes were filled with a calm understanding.

He knew they were right. He knew that he had to confront the possibility that something beyond the ordinary was happening in the city. Something that challenged his very beliefs.

They spent the next hours discussing theories, possibilities, and implications. They poured over Tim's notes, and tried to find patterns or connections.

As the night wore on, Tim's determination grew. He would not be swayed by fear or uncertainty. He would find answers. He would dig deeper, search further, and uncover the hidden secrets of the city.

But with that determination came a newfound openness, a willingness to look beyond the surface, to entertain possibilities that he would have once dismissed.

The city of Melbourne, with its vibrant culture and stunning architecture, had always fascinated Tim. But now, it was more than a fascination. It was a calling. A challenge.

The next day, Tim hit the streets with renewed vigour. He interviewed more people, researched more archives, and followed every lead. But this time, he did so with an open mind, ready to accept that the world might be more complex and wonderful than he had ever imagined.

He found himself drawn to Flinders Street Station again and again, standing at the spot where they had seen the shadow, feeling the energy of the place, trying to sense something beyond what his eyes could see.

Days turned into weeks, and the investigation became an obsession. Tim's life revolved around the mystery, and he lost himself in the search for answers.

But the deeper he went, the more questions arose. The more he learned, the less he understood.

He found records of unexplained phenomena dating back decades, stories of shadows, movements, and voices. He found people who had seen things they couldn't explain, heard things they couldn't understand.

And through it all, Tim wrestled with his beliefs, caught between the rational and the inexplicable, between the known and the unknown.

The city had revealed a side that was both exciting and terrifying. A side that challenged everything Tim had believed in.

And as he delved deeper, as he uncovered more and more, he realised that he was not just investigating a mystery. He was confronting the unseen, the unexplained, and the unimaginable.

He was on a journey that would take him beyond the boundaries of his understanding, into a world where the rules of logic and reason no longer applied.

A world where anything was possible.

And he knew, with a certainty that both thrilled and scared him, that he would never be the same again. The city had changed him, and he was changing the city.

The mystery was no longer just a story to be reported. It was a part of him, a challenge to be met, something to be uncovered.

And he was ready.

CHAPTER 3.1: A CITY'S VEIL

Tim sat in the historical section of Melbourne's State Library of Victoria, surrounded by stacks of old books and musty manuscripts. His mind was a whirlwind, still reeling from the inexplicable events that had transpired. The phenomena were beginning to form a pattern, and it was clear that the trail led into the distant past. He was now delving into the annals of Melbourne's history, seeking connections between the seemingly unexplainable occurrences and the city's cultural heritage.

Heidi was at the next table, engrossed in a volume detailing the legends and folklore of the region. Georgia and Noah were scattered elsewhere within the library, each exploring a different avenue of inquiry. Together, they were mapping a web of tales and myths that seemed to resonate with the incidents they'd witnessed.

Heidi looked up from her book, her eyes wide with astonishment. "Tim, listen to this," she called softly, not wanting to disturb the sanctity of the library. "There's a recurring theme in these stories. It talks about a thin barrier or veil that separates our world from something unknown. It's not portrayed as something supernatural, but rather as a part of the city's heritage."

Tim's interest was piqued. He leaned closer, eager to learn more. The idea of a mysterious veil seemed to connect with the shadows and whispers they had encountered.

"Let me see that," he said, reaching for the book. Heidi handed it over, pointing to the relevant passage.

The words were archaic, the language poetic, but the concept was clear. It spoke of a hidden aspect of the city, something woven into the very fabric of Melbourne's existence. A part of the land, the buildings, the people. The veil was a metaphor, a way to describe something ineffable that had been passed down through generations.

"What do you make of this, Tim?" Heidi asked, her eyes searching his face for a reaction.

He pondered the words, trying to fit them into the puzzle they were assembling.

"It's fascinating," he finally said. "This idea of a veil is not portrayed as fantasy or legend but as a historical reality. A way of understanding something complex and profound about the city."

Noah joined them, intrigued by their discussion. "You think this has something to do with what we've been experiencing?" he asked.

"I'm not sure," Tim replied, "but it's another piece of the puzzle. These legends may have a basis in reality, perhaps a way the ancient inhabitants of this land tried to make sense of something they couldn't fully comprehend."

Georgia, who had been listening from a nearby table, interjected, "These stories could provide a cultural and historical context to all of this. They're not necessarily supernatural but a part of the city's identity. Understanding them might help us figure out what's going on."

The group continued to delve into the folklore, piecing together the stories with meticulous care. The mysterious veil became a recurring theme, a concept that seemed to encapsulate the essence of their investigation. They were uncovering a part of Melbourne's soul, something hidden yet intrinsic to its character.

In the days that followed, they spoke to local historians, cultural experts, and elders who had preserved the traditions and legends of the city. They found a common thread, a belief in something more profound than mere folklore.

As Tim stood one evening, looking up at the stars from his townhouse window, he felt a new understanding dawning within him. Melbourne was more than just a place; it was a living entity, with layers of history, culture, and mystery intertwined.

He knew that their investigation was far from over, that there was still much to learn and discover. The veil was a metaphor, but it was also a guide, a path into the unknown. He realised that they were not chasing shadows or hunting ghosts, but uncovering the heart of the city itself.

Tim's skepticism had been hit with cracks by the evidence, by the connections they had uncovered. He was no longer the staunch skeptic; he was a seeker, ready to explore the depths of Melbourne's hidden heritage.

The ancient legends had become a part of their quest, not as supernatural tales, but as the soul of the city. The thin barrier, the mysterious veil, was a concept that transcended myth, linking the past to the present, the known to the unknown.

The group's investigation was only just beginning, but they were on a path that led beyond the ordinary. They were exploring the essence of Melbourne, unearthing secrets that had been buried for generations.

And somewhere, in the shadows of Flinders Street Station or in the whispering winds of the Yarra River, the veil was waiting. A doorway to something profound, a gateway to the heart of the city itself. The mystery was deepening, and Tim knew that they were on the brink of something extraordinary.

CHAPTER 3.2: HIDDEN SHADOWS

Tim felt the first twinge of suspicion as he sifted through the archives at Melbourne Town Hall. He had been searching for building permits and historical records related to Flinders Street Station, but the documents were either missing or strangely altered. Lines were redacted, dates were changed, and entire pages were seemingly misplaced.

"This doesn't make any sense," he muttered to himself, frustration creeping into his voice.

"What's wrong?" Heidi asked, glancing up from her own research.

"I can't find anything consistent about Flinders Street Station's recent renovations," Tim replied, rubbing his temples. "It's like someone has gone through these files and selectively removed or altered information."

Heidi's eyes widened as she realised the implications. "You think it's deliberate?"

"I don't know what else to think," Tim said, his mind racing. "There's a pattern here. It's too systematic to be a coincidence."

They continued their search, but the inconsistencies and gaps only multiplied. Official records that should have been readily available were missing. Eyewitness accounts from recent events near the veil's focal point were conspicuously absent.

Tim's journalistic instincts were on high alert. He knew that something significant was being hidden, and he couldn't shake the feeling that powerful forces within the city were involved.

The next day, the group set out to interview more of the city's residents, hoping to gain insight into the recent unexplained events. But their inquiries were met with resistance. Shop owners turned away, and even long-time residents seemed evasive or fearful.

"What's going on here?" Georgia asked, frustration evident in her voice. "Why won't anyone talk to us?"

"It's like they're scared," Noah observed, his eyes scanning the street.

Tim was deep in thought, piecing together the puzzle. "Or maybe they've been warned not to talk."

The realisation sent a chill down their spines. If Tim's suspicion was correct, it meant that their investigation was being monitored, possibly even obstructed.

Determined not to be deterred, Tim decided to dig deeper. He reached out to an old contact within Victoria Police, Detective Isabella Thompson, who he knew to be both reliable and discreet.

Meeting in a quiet corner of a dim cafc, Tim laid out what they had found so far. Isabella listened intently, his expression growing increasingly concerned.

"I've noticed some strange things myself," Isabella finally admitted. "Closed cases that shouldn't have been closed, evidence that doesn't add up. I thought I was just being paranoid, but hearing what you've found, I'm not so sure."

"You think there's a cover-up?" Tim asked, his voice barely above a whisper.

"I don't know what else to call it," Isabella said, shaking her head. "Someone, or something, is actively suppressing information."

The meeting ended with a promise from Isabella to help in any way she could. Tim left the cafe with a heavy heart, the weight of what they had uncovered settling on his shoulders.

The investigation was no longer just about ancient legends and mysterious occurrences. They were now delving into a realm of modern conspiracy, facing opponents that were all too real and potentially very dangerous.

In the days that followed, the group worked tirelessly, following leads, connecting dots, and uncovering a web of deception that spanned the city's government, law enforcement, and even some influential business leaders.

The veil, it seemed, was not just a part of Melbourne's cultural heritage. It was a living, breathing entity, and there were those within the city who were not only aware of its existence but were actively working to control or suppress it.

As Tim stood in his house looking towards the city, he knew that they were on the brink of something monumental. The shadows were deepening, the stakes were rising, and the mystery was evolving into a battle between the known and the unknown, between those who sought to uncover secrets and those who wished to keep them hidden.

The veil was no longer just a metaphor or a legend; it was a doorway to a reality that transcended ordinary understanding. The question was, were they ready for what lay beyond the veil? Were they prepared to face the hidden shadows that were now stretching out to touch them?

Only time would tell, but one thing was certain: the investigation had taken a turn, and there was no going back. The trail was leading them down a path of intrigue and danger, and they were following it without hesitation.

CHAPTER 3.3: THE PERCEPTUAL BOUNDARY

The following weeks were a whirlwind of interviews, research, and discovery. Tim and his group dug deep into the city's archives, visited obscure libraries, and managed to find a handful of older residents who were willing to discuss the so-called veil.

The accounts were both fascinating and unsettling. The veil was described as a perceptual boundary, a place where the ordinary laws of physics and reality seemed to waver and bend. It was not just an ancient legend, but a phenomenon that had been observed over centuries.

One elderly woman, Mrs. O'Leary, recounted a story from her youth. Her voice quivered in her Irish accent as she spoke of a summer's evening when she had seen the veil manifest in a local park.

"It was like looking through a shimmering curtain," she said, her eyes distant. "I saw colours I can't describe, shapes that twisted and danced. It was beautiful, but it made me feel so small, so insignificant."

Another interviewee, a retired historian named Mr. Sullivan, provided insight into the cultural context. He explained that the veil had been part of the city's folklore for generations, connected to specific locations and times.

"Some say it's a gateway to another world," he mused, stroking his white beard.

"Others believe it's a reflection of our own subconscious fears and desires. But all agree that it's real, and that it has the power to both enthral and terrify."

These interviews were a goldmine of information, but Tim struggled to reconcile the accounts with his rational worldview. He was a journalist, trained to seek evidence and logic, but the veil defied explanation.

"It's like trying to describe a dream," Noah said one night, as they poured over their notes. "You can use words, but they never quite capture the essence."

"But it's not a dream," Georgia interjected. "It's a physical phenomenon. It can be measured, analysed."

"Can it?" Heidi asked, raising an eyebrow. "We're dealing with something that seems to exist outside the normal bounds of science."

They debated long into the night, grappling with the contradictions and ambiguities. The veil was elusive, a paradox that seemed to exist in the shadows of reason.

Tim found himself drawn to the descriptions of the veil's beauty, the way it played with light and colour, the way it seemed to beckon and call. He imagined standing at the edge of reality, peering into the unknown, feeling both awe and terror.

Yet, the rational part of his mind resisted. He knew that there had to be an explanation, a scientific basis for what they were uncovering. The veil could not be a mere fantasy or delusion. There had to be a reason, a cause, a truth that could be unearthed.

He began to approach the phenomenon as a puzzle, a complex riddle that required a careful and methodical approach. He started mapping the known locations of the veil's manifestations, looking for patterns and connections.

"We need to understand its nature," he told the group, his voice filled with determination. "We need to break it down, analyse its components, figure out its rules."

"But what if there are no rules?" Heidi asked, her voice gentle. "What if the veil is something that transcends our understanding?"

"Then we'll find a way to understand it," Tim replied, his eyes filled with resolve. "We'll find a way to bridge the gap between what's known and what's unknown."

They continued their research with renewed vigour., uncovering more accounts, more descriptions, more pieces of the puzzle.

They consulted scientists, psychologists, and even artists, seeking to understand the veil from every possible angle.

The more they learned, the more complex and intriguing the veil became. It was a phenomenon that seemed to exist at the intersection of science and art, reason and emotion, the physical and the metaphysical.

As the days turned into weeks, Tim's fascination grew into an obsession. The veil was no longer just a story, but a challenge, a mystery that demanded to be solved.

He knew that he was on the brink of something profound, something that could change not only his understanding of the world but also his understanding of himself.

The veil had become a mirror, reflecting his own doubts and desires, his own struggle to reconcile the rational and the irrational. He knew that the path ahead would be filled with twists and turns, doubts and revelations, but he was no longer afraid.

He was ready to step beyond the perceptual boundary, to explore the spaces between reality and illusion, to uncover the hidden layers of existence.

CHAPTER 3.4: HIDDEN CONNECTIONS

The morning sun was still shy, casting a soft light through the window. Tim, Georgia, and the rest of the group were huddled around the dining table at Georgia's city apartment, where she lived with Noah. Surrounded by an array of old books, handwritten notes, faded maps, and photographs from their investigation, they were deep into trying to decipher the patterns and connections between the veil and the city's history.

Their faces showed the wear of an all-nighter, but their eyes sparkled with relentless determination. Something about this investigation had consumed them, igniting a fire that transcended mere intellectual pursuit.

During a brief pause in the conversation, as Georgia prepared some much-needed coffee, Tim's eyes were drawn to an ornate silver locket on a nearby shelf. It was intricately designed, with delicate engravings and a small sapphire embedded in the centre.

"What's this, Georgia?" Tim asked, picking up the locket and examining it closely. His journalist's instincts were buzzing, sensing that this was more than a mere trinket.

"Oh, that?" Georgia said, glancing over. "I'm told it's a family heirloom. Grandma gave it to me when I was little, but I never really paid much attention to it."

Tim continued to study the locket, feeling a strange pull towards it. The engravings were more than mere decorations; they were symbols, patterns that he had seen before in their research.

"Wait a minute," he said, his voice filled with a mix of excitement and disbelief. "This symbol... I've seen it in some of the ancient texts we've been studying. I'm sure it's connected to the veil."

The room went silent as they all absorbed the implications. The locket was not just a family keepsake; it was a tangible connection between Tim and Georgia's family history and the veil.

"What does this mean?" Georgia asked, her voice filled with a mixture of wonder and trepidation.

"It means that our family might have been involved with the veil," Tim replied, his mind racing. "There's a possibility that they knew something about its nature."

They began to dig deeper, pulling out books and cross-referencing information. They found historical records that mentioned their family name in connection with ancient ceremonies and rituals that seemed to align with the veil's manifestations.

The realisation was both thrilling and unsettling. The story had taken a personal turn, and the connection between their family history and the city's mystery added a new dimension to their quest for understanding.

They spent the rest of the day and deep into the night studying the locket, searching for more clues, and what the markings might mean. They found hidden compartments and inscriptions that hinted at a deeper story, a narrative that intertwined Tim and Georgia's family with the city's history.

As the hours wore on, they uncovered stories of love and loss, triumph and tragedy, all linked to the veil's enigmatic presence. They learned about ancestors who had sought to understand the perceptual boundary, who had been both drawn to its beauty and haunted by its terror.

The veil was no longer just a random phenomenon that they had stumbled across; it was part of their heritage. A link to their own family that they had to understand.

The excitement of discovery was tempered by a growing sense of responsibility. They were treading on sacred ground, unearthing secrets that had been buried for such a long time. But they were driven by a need to know, a desire to understand the connection that had been revealed.

With the locket as their guide, they were ready to explore the spaces between reality and illusion, to unravel the ties that bound them to their past, their city, and each other.

The quest had become personal, and they were prepared to embrace it, knowing that the road ahead would be filled with challenges and surprises. With a newfound sense of purpose, they looked to the future, ready to continue their journey, to forge a path through the unknown, guided by the hidden connections that had been revealed.

As they finally settled down for a few hours of rest, they knew that they were finally starting to reach the point of making sense of things.

CHAPTER 3.5: A SHATTERED UNDERSTANDING

The sound of rain continued to beat on the windows, but inside Tim's townhouse, the group was engulfed in a silence thick with anticipation. Spread across the dining table were documents, maps, photos, a worn-out journal that had belonged to Tim's great-grandfather, and Georgia's haunting family heirloom that had ignited their discovery.

The afternoon sun was gone, leaving the room bathed in the soft glow of table lamps. Shadows danced across the faces of Tim, Georgia, Heidi, and Noah as they pored over the research material.

Tim's mind was a whirlpool, teetering on the edge of something profound. He had always sought facts, evidence, concrete explanations. But the day had been filled with contradictions, inexplicable phenomena, and now a connection between his family and the phenomenon known as the veil.

Georgia was absorbed in translating an old letter, using a magnifying glass to decipher the faded handwriting. Her brow furrowed as she navigated the archaic language. Noah had meticulously pieced together the timeline, creating a flowchart that connected the legends with actual events. Heidi, had cross-referenced the ancient tales with scientific theories, attempting to find a logical explanation.

A shiver ran down Tim's spine as he reached for the journal, his great-grandfather's words speaking across the generations. The descriptions of the veil, its connection to specific places, the sensations – they were all eerily similar to what Tim himself had experienced.

He turned a page, and his heart stopped.

A sketch, crudely drawn but unmistakable, depicted a man standing at the edge of what seemed to be the veil. A hand extended, fingers almost touching the shimmering barrier. The face of the man was obscured, but the details of his clothing, his posture, the surroundings were all too familiar.

It was him. Tim.

The shock was immediate, like a jolt of electricity. He could feel his pulse in his throat as he looked up, meeting Georgia's eyes. She had stopped reading, drawn by the change in his breathing.

"What is it, Tim?" she asked, concern etching her face.

"It's me," Tim whispered, pointing at the sketch. "This... this is me."

Heidi and Noah gathered around, their faces reflecting the shock and disbelief that Tim felt.

"But how...?" Noah stammered.

"I don't know," Tim replied, his voice trembling. "But it's all here. My great-grandfather wrote about someone in our family who could perceive the veil, interact with it. And this sketch... it's as if he saw me."

They spent the next hour discussing the implications, each person grappling with their emotions. Fear, excitement, bewilderment, they all mingled in a cocktail of uncertainty.

"What does this mean, Tim?" Georgia finally asked, her voice almost a plea. "What does this mean for us?"

"I don't know," Tim said again, his mind racing. "But we've stumbled upon something far bigger than we ever imagined. And it's not just about uncovering a hidden secret; it's personal now. It's about understanding who we are and what this means for our family."

They explored every angle, from the possibility of genetic memory to the nature of time itself. The room was filled with hypotheses, theories, questions that seemed to multiply with each passing moment.

He looked at the sketch again, the drawn figure reaching for the unknown. His great-grandfather's words echoed in his mind, hinting at a path, a destiny, a role that Tim had never sought but now seemed thrust upon him.

As the night wore on, the veil's existence became more tangible. It was not just a legend; it was a part of him. It had always been there, lurking in the shadows, waiting for him to discover it. The evidence was undeniable, the connection between him and the ancient legends irrefutable.

They took turns reading from the journal, delving deeper into the family's history. The stories were vivid, filled with accounts of visions, premonitions, dreams that transcended time. They all seemed to point to a unique ability that had been passed down through generations.

As the realisation settled, a chilling thought crept into Tim's mind. If his family's history was intertwined with the veil, what else lay hidden? What dangers and responsibilities did this newfound knowledge carry? Or was it that he was meant to reveal the secrets of the veil to the wider community?

The questions were many, the answers elusive. One thing was certain, though; Tim's pursuit of the truth had led him down a path from which there was no turning back.

And as the rain continued to pour outside, Tim felt a profound change within himself. A door had been opened, a secret revealed, and his life would never be the same again.

The time of understanding had been shattered, and a new, uncertain path lay ahead. The veil had shown its presence, and the mysteries that lay beyond were calling him, beckoning him into the unknown.

CHAPTER 4.1: UNRAVELLING ROOTS

Tim's mind swirled as he stared at the worn family photo in his hand, a snapshot from a past he thought he knew. The backdrop of the old family estate had always been just a part of his childhood scenery, but now it loomed large, filled with questions and shadows. Georgia sat beside him, equally lost in thought, her fingers playing with an old locket that once belonged to their grandmother.

"I've walked those halls a thousand times," Tim whispered, more to himself than anyone else. "Why does it feel so foreign now?"

Georgia looked up from the locket. "Maybe because we've never seen it through this lens before. Everything has changed, Tim."

Their friend Noah, who had been quietly flipping through an old family album, nodded. "This place, your family—it's all woven into the fabric of this city and its legends. The veil... It's like it's calling to you."

Tim's heart pounded at the thought. The word 'veil' had taken on a new significance, a metaphor for a boundary that he seemed destined to cross. He could no longer ignore the peculiar sense that there was something more to his family's history and his own place in it.

The next few days were a whirlwind of activity. Tim, Georgia, and Noah delved into archives, dug through dusty boxes, and sought out distant relatives who might hold a key to the past. They travelled throughout Melbourne, visiting places that were once a part of Tim's childhood but now held new meaning.

They found themselves standing in front of the old family estate in Cranbourne North, a busy suburb in the south-east corner of Melbourne. Its grand structure cast long shadows that seemed to reach out to them. Tim's memory painted the place with laughter, picnics, and warm summer days, but those images were now layered with a sense of foreboding.

A visit to their elderly Aunt Clare brought more revelations. Though frail and forgetful, her eyes sparkled when Tim mentioned the veil.

"Oh yes," she said, her voice a soft tremor. "Your great-grandfather spoke of it. A place where the world bends, where dreams and reality touch. He said it was both a gift and a burden."

Her words hung in the air, and Tim could feel a chill running down his spine. Was this what he had sensed all along? Was he somehow tied to this phenomenon?

The exploration into their family's past opened doors that had long been sealed. Memories resurfaced, some warm and comforting, others unsettling. Tim recalled a recurring dream he had as a child, where he stood at the edge of a shimmering boundary, something beautiful yet terrifying just beyond his reach.

Georgia, too, felt a connection, a pull toward something they were yet to fully grasp. She remembered stories their grandmother used to tell, fairytales that now seemed like allegories for something profound and real.

Days turned into weeks, and the four friends found themselves immersed in a world they never expected. The city, with its rich history and culture, was no longer just a backdrop to their lives. It was a living, breathing entity, holding secrets that seemed to beckon them.

Yet, the more they uncovered, the more elusive the true nature of the veil became. Was it a physical place, a state of mind, or something beyond comprehension? The answer danced just out of reach, like a mirage that shifted with every step they took.

Tim's rational mind wrestled with the inexplicable, caught between the concrete evidence and the ethereal nature of their discovery. He felt a calling, a destiny he couldn't ignore, but understanding it was like trying to grasp smoke.

As they sat around the table one night, doing the usual act of studying old maps and documents, Tim looked up, his face etched with determination and wonder.

"We're on the edge of something incredible," he said, his voice filled with a conviction that surprised even him. "We can't stop now. We must find the answers."

Georgia reached over and squeezed his hand, her face mirroring his resolve. "We will, Tim. We're in this together."

They knew they were only scratching the surface, that the journey ahead was filled with unknowns. But the connection to the veil had become personal, a part of who they were and who they were meant to be. The mystery was no longer just a puzzle to be solved; it was a calling, a quest that had become their own.

In the quiet of the night, as Melbourne slept, Tim stood by the window, his reflection mingling with the lights. He felt a presence, a connection to something greater, and he knew that their discovery was only the beginning.

The veil was real, and it was calling to him. Its nature remained elusive, but its existence was now part of his very being. Tim's connection to the veil was not just a link to his family's past; it was a pathway to a new understanding, a bridge to a world he was only beginning to comprehend.

Tim knew that he was stepping into the unknown, guided by a force that transcended time and space. The veil was no longer just a legend; it was a reality, a mystery that he was destined to unravel. The questions remained, but the pursuit had become a part of him, a journey he knew he must take.

He looked out towards the city, his city, and felt a shiver of anticipation. The veil was there, somewhere, waiting for him to find it. The path was unclear, the destination unknown, but he was ready. Tim's eyes sparkled with a sense of purpose, and he knew that he was on the brink of something extraordinary.

The adventure had truly begun.

CHAPTER 4.2: SECRETS UNVEILED

The room was filled with the musty scent of aged paper and the gentle hum of Tim's laptop as he logged into the city's historical archive website. His heart pounded with anticipation, each keystroke echoing the rhythm of discovery. Around him, Georgia, Noah, and Heidi immersed themselves in books, photographs, and documents, their focus intense.

They had embarked on a journey into their family's past, spurred by the connection between Tim and Georgia's lineage and the veil—a phenomenon both wondrous and mysterious. It was a path fraught with uncertainty, but the allure of the unknown beckoned them forward.

"Hey, take a look at this," Georgia called from across the room, her voice breaking through Tim's concentration. He glanced up to find her holding an old photograph, her eyes wide with astonishment.

Curiosity ignited, Tim moved to her side and gasped at what he saw. There, in black and white, was their great-grandfather, standing beside an ornate door, engraved with symbols they had seen in other references to the veil.

"Noah, Heidi, come see this!" Tim exclaimed, his voice trembling with excitement. His friends gathered around, their expressions mirroring his surprise.

Heidi was the first to speak. "This might be a clue. We should find out where that door is located. It could lead to something significant."

The photograph was merely the beginning. As they delved deeper into the family's archives, they uncovered a treasure trove of information. Letters exchanged between ancestors, journals filled with observations and theories, even sketches and maps—all pointing to a deeper connection between Tim and Georgia's family and the veil.

Continuing reading through his great-grandfather's old journal, Tim found an entry that described experiments conducted on the veil, exploring its properties and manifestations. The words were filled with a mix of awe and caution, expressing a profound respect for something beyond ordinary comprehension.

But the path to understanding was not without its obstacles. Some documents were coded, their meanings obscured by a cipher only those initiated into the family's secrets would understand. Others were hidden away, only to be revealed through careful and patient exploration.

The connections were complex and rich, painting a picture of ancestors who were researchers, guardians, and perhaps even exploiters of the veil. They had stood at the threshold of a world where the ordinary laws of physics seemed to waver, where beauty and terror intertwined.

The implications were both thrilling and unsettling. Tim's family was not merely spectators to the veil; they were entwined with it. They were part of its history.

But along with the wonder, there were also shadows. Some accounts hinted at manipulations, perhaps even exploitation of the veil for personal gain. These allegations were subtle, buried in cryptic messages, but they were there, nagging at Tim's conscience.

"How deep does this go?" he wondered aloud, a knot of uncertainty forming in his stomach.

Heidi placed a comforting hand on his shoulder. "We're unearthing history, Tim. Some of it may be dark, but it's essential to understand the whole picture."

The group painstakingly continued piecing together the history. The more they uncovered, the more complex the puzzle became. The veil was a double-edged sword, a source of beauty and potential danger, and it had shaped their family's legacy in ways they couldn't have imagined.

Ethical questions began to emerge, casting doubt over some of the family's actions. Was it right to experiment with something so powerful and unknown? Was the family's involvement a quest for knowledge or an unbridled ambition for power?

The more Tim learned, the more he grappled with his family's legacy. He felt both honoured and burdened, knowing that he was part of something much bigger. He looked out the window towards the city that he had always been so familiar with, seeing it now with new eyes.

The room was quiet as the group absorbed the magnitude of what they had learned. The secrets of the past had been unveiled, opening doors to new possibilities and challenges. Tim's journey had taken a personal turn, and he knew that the path ahead would be filled with discovery, reflection, and perhaps even redemption.

They had unearthed long-hidden secrets, and the echoes of the past resonated with a newfound clarity. Tim's connection to the veil was no longer a mere hypothesis; it was a tangible reality, woven into the fabric of his very being.

As he sat back in his chair, lost in thought, he realised once again that the veil was calling to him, a whisper from the annals of history. A challenge, a responsibility, a mystery that only they could unravel. The secrets of his family and the veil were waiting to be discovered, and he was determined to uncover them, no matter where the journey would lead him.

CHAPTER 4.3: BONDS AND TENSIONS

The pursuit of the veil had brought Tim, Georgia, Noah, and Heidi together. Now, as they entered the next phase of their investigation, their different backgrounds, skills, and perspectives melded into a dynamic synergy. They were united by a shared sense of purpose, each one contributing to the unravelling of the complex fabric of the veil's history.

But as the mystery deepened, the stakes grew higher, and the shadows of personal ambition and conflicting morals began to loom over the group.

Heidi approached the veil with scholarly curiosity. She sought to place it within the context of human history, understanding its role in shaping cultures and beliefs.

Noah was fascinated by the potential applications of the veil. He saw it as a gateway to undiscovered scientific principles, an opportunity to expand the boundaries of human knowledge.

Georgia's connection was more visceral. The family link, the secrets uncovered, had stirred something profound within her. She was drawn to the spiritual aspect, the intangible resonance that seemed to vibrate within her very soul.

And then there was Tim, caught at the intersection of fascination, responsibility, and fear. His personal connection to the veil, the implications for his family's legacy, weighed heavily on him. He was both awed and haunted by the mysteries they were uncovering.

Their different viewpoints fuelled lively discussions, debates that often stretched late into the night. At times, the interplay of ideas led to groundbreaking insights. They found connections between ancient texts and modern theories, pieced together fragments of history, and began to discern the outlines of the veil's influence on human civilisation.

But the tensions were also building.

"What if we're meddling with something we don't fully understand?" Tim questioned one evening, his voice tinged with unease.

Noah's eyes flashed with excitement. "But that's the essence of discovery, Tim! Think of the possibilities, the doors we could open!"

"I agree with Noah," Heidi chimed in. "We're on the brink of something incredible. This could reshape our understanding of history, of reality itself."

Georgia looked thoughtful. "But at what cost? What if there's a reason this has been hidden for so long?"

The room fell silent. She had a point.

As the days passed, the cracks began to show. Tim's caution clashed with Noah's enthusiasm. Heidi's academic approach grated against Georgia's intuitive connection. The debates grew more heated, the disagreements more personal.

And yet, through it all, their camaraderie endured. They were bound by a shared journey, a collective quest that transcended their differences.

Tim found himself turning to Georgia for support. As siblings, they shared not only a family connection to the veil but also a deeper understanding of each other's fears and hopes. Their late-night talks became a balm for Tim's anxiety, a space for reflection and empathy.

Heidi and Noah, too, found solace in each other's company. Their intellectual curiosity and passion for discovery drew them closer, forging a bond that went beyond mere friendship.

Despite the tensions, the group's dynamic interplay led to new understandings of the veil. They mapped its historical footprint, traced its influence on art, science, and religion, and began to glimpse its multifaceted nature.

But as they drew closer to the heart of the mystery, the personal stakes grew higher. The veil was no longer a distant fantasy; it was part of them, woven into their lives, their dreams, their very identities.

The room was charged with an unspoken tension as they gathered around the table one evening, each lost in their thoughts. The excitement of discovery was tempered by the realisation that they were venturing into uncharted territory, treading a fine line between wonder and danger.

They were a team, bound by a shared quest, yet also divided by their unique perspectives. The veil had brought them together, but it also threatened to pull them apart.

Tim looked around at his friends, his family, feeling both grateful and apprehensive. They had come so far, yet the journey was far from over. The veil's allure was irresistible, its secrets beckoning them onward, but the path ahead was fraught with uncertainty.

He knew that they were on the brink of something profound, something that would challenge not only their understanding of the world but also their relationships with each other. The veil had become more than a mystery; it was a mirror, reflecting their deepest desires, fears, and conflicts.

As they delved deeper into its complexities, they would have to confront not only the veil's unusual nature but also the truths within themselves. The road ahead was uncharted, filled with promise and peril, and they would have to navigate it together, forging new bonds and facing new tensions.

The pursuit of the veil had become a journey of self-discovery, a path that would test their resolve, their friendship, and their very sense of who they were. The mystery had become personal, and the stakes had never been higher.

CHAPTER 4.4: AN UNEARTHLY ENCOUNTER

The day had been filled with intense research, and the four of them sat exhausted in the dimly lit room, surrounded by scattered papers and artefacts. Tim, Georgia, Heidi, and Noah had reached a point in their investigation where the theoretical had to give way to the experiential. They needed to connect with the veil, to somehow touch it or feel it.

They decided to visit one of the locations tied to their family's history, a place where the veil's influence had been documented before. It was an ancient site, its stones worn smooth by centuries, hidden away in a clearing in Dandenong Ranges National Park.

As they approached the location, they could sense a subtle shift in the air, a vibrational quality that seemed to permeate everything. It was as if the very ground beneath them resonated with a frequency that spoke to something deep within their souls.

Tim felt a chill run down his spine. His connection to the veil had always been a theoretical concept, something read in dusty books or whispered by old relatives. But now, it was tangible, something he could feel.

Georgia's eyes widened, her artistic sensibility picking up colours and textures that seemed out of place, a surreal overlay on the natural landscape.

Heidi's analytical mind raced, trying to categorise and understand the phenomena, yet finding no easy explanations.

And Noah's technological curiosity was piqued by the interaction of the environment with their electronic devices, strange malfunctions, and unexpected readings.

They stood at the edge of the clearing, each lost in their perceptions, feeling the pull of something unseen, something powerful and profound.

"Can you feel that?" Tim whispered, his voice almost lost in the gentle rustle of the leaves.

"It's like a melody, a song I've heard before," Georgia replied.

"It doesn't make sense," Heidi murmured, her brow furrowed. "But it's real. I can feel it too."

Noah simply nodded, staring intently at his handheld device, its screen displaying erratic patterns.

They moved closer, drawn by an inexplicable force, a magnetic pull that seemed to emanate from the very heart of the clearing.

The air grew thicker, charged with a palpable energy that prickled their skin and sent shivers through their bodies.

And then, without warning, it happened.

A manifestation of the veil, a shimmering distortion in the air that seemed to ripple and dance, like a mirage. It was there, and yet not there, a paradox that defied explanation.

They stood transfixed, each perceiving the phenomenon in a unique way.

Tim saw flashes of history, images of his ancestors, echoes of voices that spoke of duty and legacy.

Georgia felt a surge of creativity, visions of artworks and poems, a symphony of ideas that transcended time and space.

Heidi experienced a connection to humanity, a thread that linked cultures and civilisations, a tapestry of shared experience.

And Noah, ever the scientist, saw equations and algorithms, a code that hinted at the underlying structure of reality.

The moment stretched, time seeming to lose its meaning as they were engulfed in the experience, each lost in their perceptions, yet also connected, sharing something profound and life-altering.

And then, as suddenly as it had appeared, the manifestation receded, the ripple in the air smoothing out, the clearing returning to its natural state. The unseen static feeling in the air was gone.

They stood in stunned silence, each trying to come to terms with what they had just experienced.

"What was that?" Georgia finally whispered, her voice trembling.

"I don't know," Tim replied, his eyes wide. "But it was real. It was the veil."

Heidi simply nodded, her mind still racing, struggling to make sense of the experience.

Noah looked up from his device, his face pale. "Whatever it was, it's beyond anything I've ever seen."

They made their way back to their temporary base, each lost in thought, the experience replaying in their minds.

The encounter with the veil had solidified their commitment to uncovering the bizarre mystery. It had transcended their initial relationships, forging a bond that went beyond friendship or collaboration.

They were connected now, not just by a shared goal but by a shared experience, something profound and inexplicable that had touched them all.

As they settled down that night, the event still fresh in their minds, they knew that their journey had reached a new level of intensity. The veil was no longer just a mystery to be solved; it was a calling, a destiny that they were compelled to follow.

They were united, not just by curiosity or ambition but by something deeper, a connection that transcended words and explanations.

They were a team, bound by a shared experience, driven by a shared purpose.

And they knew, with a certainty that defied logic, that they were on the right path, that the veil was calling them, guiding them towards a discovery that was both terrifying and beautiful.

They were explorers, venturing into the unknown, driven by a force they could not fully understand but could no longer deny.

The veil had chosen them, and they would follow, wherever it led, whatever the cost. It was personal now, the stakes higher than ever before, and they would face it together, as one.

CHAPTER 4.5: REFLECTION AND RESOLVE

In the quiet solitude of the night, with the events of the day still reverberating in his mind, Tim found himself unable to sleep. He sat by the window, the soft glow of the moon illuminating his thoughtful face.

The veil had touched him in ways he never thought possible. It was more than a historical artefact or a family legend; it was a living presence, something that had reached out and connected with him on a deep, personal level.

He thought about his ancestors, those who had been involved with the veil in the past. What had they known? What had they felt? Were they guided by the same calling that now tugged at his heart?

Tim's beliefs had been shaken. The veil had shown him things that transcended logic and reason, things that spoke to a deeper understanding of reality. It had opened doors in his mind, revealing pathways that he never knew existed.

He felt a sense of responsibility, a duty to explore those pathways, to follow where they led. The veil was not just a part of his family's history; it was a part of him. It had chosen him, and he knew that he could not turn away.

Meanwhile, Georgia was in her room, her sketchbook filled with images inspired by the encounter with the veil. She had seen colours and shapes that she was sure did not exist in this world, visions that danced at the edge of her consciousness. She felt a surge of creativity, a desire to capture the essence of what she had experienced.

Her role in the unfolding mystery was clear. She was the artist, the visionary, the one who could give form to the formless, translate the abstract into something that others could see and understand. The veil had spoken to her, and she would try to make sense of it with her art.

Heidi was at her laptop, her mind racing with possibilities. The veil was a puzzle, a complex system that defied easy explanation. But she was determined to understand, to find the patterns and connections that would unlock its secrets.

Her analytical mind was engaged, her intellectual curiosity sparked. She was the scientist, the thinker, the one who would dissect and analyse, who would seek to understand the how and the why. She's the one who should be able to provide a general explanation of things based on scientific theories, but she was perplexed. The veil had challenged her, right to her limits and potentially beyond.

Noah was in his makeshift lab, surrounded by gadgets and technology. The veil had interacted with his devices in ways that he still couldn't fully comprehend. It had shown him that there was more to the world than circuits and code, that there were dimensions beyond the physical.

He felt a sense of wonder, a desire to explore those dimensions, to find the underlying structure that connected everything. He was the technologist, the one who would bridge the gap between the seen and the unseen. The veil had intrigued him, and he would follow where it led.

The next morning, they gathered together, each having spent the night reflecting on their experiences, their roles, their connections to the veil.

"I want to understand," Heidi said, her voice firm. "I want to know what the veil is, what it means."

They clasped hands, a symbol of their unity, their commitment to each other and to the mystery that had brought them together.

The chapter of their lives had ended, and a new one was beginning. The veil had called, and they had answered. They were on a journey, a journey that would take them to places they never imagined, that would challenge their beliefs, their understanding, their very sense of reality.

They would follow the path, wherever it led, whatever the cost.

The mystery was theirs to unravel, and they would not stop until they found their answers.

CHAPTER 5.1: AN UNEXPECTED INSIGHT

Noah was fixated on his screens, his mind piecing together patterns and whispers hidden within the data. His fingers danced across the keyboard as Tim, Georgia, and Heidi looked on, intrigued by his intense focus.

"It's like I can feel it," Noah murmured, not entirely aware he was speaking. "The veil... It's trying to say something."

"You've been saying that for a while now," Georgia noted, her voice soft, yet laced with concern. "But what do you mean exactly?"

Noah paused, still fixed on the screens, a frown creasing his brow. "It's like a melody. But it's fragmented. If we could just find the missing piece, I think we'd understand so much more."

Tim approached the screens, the connections forming in his mind. "What if the missing piece isn't in the data? What if it's in the approach?"

They all turned to him, and he continued, "We've been looking at this scientifically, historically, and even artistically. But what if we're missing a philosophical aspect? A moral or ethical angle?"

Heidi was intrigued. "That could make sense. The veil isn't just a phenomenon; it's an entity with its own rules and principles. We need to understand its nature, not just its mechanics."

The room was filled with a sudden energy, a clarity that seemed to spark new ideas and insights. They began to explore different philosophical concepts, diving into ancient texts and moral dilemmas.

The search led them to the writings of forgotten philosophers, scholars who had pondered the nature of existence, the connection between worlds, and the ethical responsibilities of those who tread the line between them.

Among the dusty pages, they found mentions of the veil, described in poetic language, hinting at its grandeur and its mystery. But more importantly, they discovered a moral code, a set of principles that seemed to govern interaction with the veil.

"Look at this," Heidi said, pointing to a passage in an old manuscript. "It speaks of respect, understanding, and humility. It's as if the veil demands these virtues from those who seek to know it."

Georgia, her artistic mind finding beauty in the words, added, "It's like a harmonious kind of dance."

Noah felt a resonance with these principles. "This is it," he declared, his voice filled with conviction. "This is what we've been missing. We need to approach the veil with these virtues, not just as a puzzle to be solved."

They spent days delving into these ethical concepts, intertwining them with their scientific understanding, their historical research, and their personal experiences.

The atmosphere was charged with anticipation, the excitement palpable as they felt themselves drawing closer to the veil, understanding it in a way they never had before.

They conducted new experiments, guided by the principles they had uncovered. They approached the veil with reverence, humility, and an open mind, seeking not to conquer it but to understand it.

And the veil responded.

They felt it in the data, in the readings, and in the very air around them. The veil was opening up, revealing itself in ways that were profound and beautiful.

Noah, in particular, seemed to become one with the investigation, his connection deepening, his understanding growing. He was like a musician who had finally found the right tune, playing it with grace and passion.

They recorded their findings, their insights, and their experiences, knowing that they were on the verge of something extraordinary.

But they also recognised the responsibility that came with this knowledge. The veil was not a mere curiosity; it was a living reality, with its own demands and expectations.

They were a team, driven by a shared purpose, a shared passion, and a shared understanding.

And they knew that they were closing in on the truth, guided by a wisdom that was as old as time itself.

The veil was no longer a distant concept; it was a living presence, a challenge, and an invitation.

CHAPTER 5.2: THE TRAGIC EXPERIMENT

The air was thick with anticipation as the group prepared for what would be a groundbreaking experiment. Noah's unique sensitivity to the veil had provided them with an extraordinary insight, leading to a breakthrough in their understanding.

They had set up their equipment back in the same clearing in Dandenong Ranges National Park, a place where the veil's presence was especially strong. The was filled with computers, sensors, and other high-tech devices, all surrounding the central point where they had seen the veil appear on their last visit.

"Noah, are you sure about this?" Tim asked, his voice tinged with concern. "This is uncharted territory. We don't fully understand what we're dealing with."

Noah looked at Tim, looking more determined than ever. "I've never been more certain of anything in my life. The veil is calling to me, Tim. I can feel it. It wants us to know, to understand."

Georgia, standing by a console filled with dials and screens, chimed in, "We've taken every precaution. All safety measures are in place."

Tim looked around the area, then back at Noah. "Alright. Let's do this."

The experiment began with a series of controlled tests, slowly escalating in intensity. Each member of the group played a crucial role, monitoring different aspects of the phenomenon.

Noah stood at the centre, acting as a conduit, a bridge between the veil and their reality. His connection was more profound than ever, a bond that transcended mere scientific curiosity.

He began to describe what he was sensing, his voice steady, his words painting a vivid picture of something beautiful and incomprehensible.

"It's like a river," he said, his voice filled with awe. "A river of light and sound, flowing through time and space. It's alive, Tim. It's conscious. I can see and feel it!"

The data was coming in fast, the readings off the charts. They were getting results that were beyond anything they had anticipated.

Then something changed.

A sudden spike in the readings, a fluctuation that was erratic and unpredictable.

"Noah, something's wrong," Georgia called out, her voice filled with alarm.

"I feel it," Noah replied, his voice tense. "Something's happening. The veil... It's reacting."

"What do we do?" Heidi asked, panic creeping into her voice.

"Shut it down!" Tim yelled, moving towards the controls.

But it was too late.

A blinding flash of light filled the clearing, a sound like thunder echoing through the air. The equipment sparked and sizzled, screens going dark.

And then, silence.

When the light faded, they found Noah lying on the floor, his body still, his eyes wide and unseeing.

Not moving. Not reacting. He was gone.

They were stunned, disbelief and shock washing over them. The experiment had gone horribly wrong, the veil reacting in a way they had never anticipated.

They called for help, the area soon filled with emergency personnel. The equipment was examined, but nobody could find an explanation what had happened.

Noah's death was ruled an accident, a tragic result of an experiment gone awry. But the details were ambiguous, the evidence inconclusive.

There were whispers, speculations about what had really happened. Some said that Noah had gone too far, that he had touched something he was not meant to touch. Others believed that the veil had claimed him, a price for their intrusion. The rumours spread.

The group was devastated but determined. They knew that Noah would want them to continue, to uncover the secrets he had died trying to understand.

They gathered in their research facility, a sombre mood hanging over them. Tim looked at the others, his eyes filled with resolve.

"We owe it to Noah to find the answers," he said, his voice filled with conviction. "We can't let his death be in vain."

They all nodded, their commitment to the investigation stronger than ever.

But they also knew that they were venturing into the unknown, that the veil was more complex and more dangerous than they had ever imagined.

The tragedy had left them with more questions than answers, the mystery deepening, the stakes higher than ever.

They were in uncharted territory, facing a phenomenon that was beyond their comprehension.

But they were driven by a purpose, a quest for understanding that transcended mere scientific curiosity.

They knew that they were on the brink of something extraordinary, a discovery that could change everything.

And they knew that they had to continue, to honour Noah's memory and to fulfil the promise of their investigation.

The veil had shown them a glimpse of its power, its majesty, and its danger.

But they were not deterred.

They were determined to unravel its secrets, to unlock its mysteries, and to find the answers they sought.

No matter what it took. No matter the cost.

The investigation was far from over. They were not going to give up now.

CHAPTER 5.3: UNSETTLED REFLECTIONS

The days following Noah's death were a blur of mixed emotions and unsettling thoughts. The group had lost a dear friend and a vital part of their investigation, though the pursuit of understanding continued, driven now by an unspoken agreement that the answers were a tribute to Noah's memory.

Tim, in particular, struggled with a heavy burden of guilt. He found himself replaying the events of that tragic day over and over in his mind, questioning his decisions, second-guessing his actions. Could he have done something differently? Had his relentless drive to uncover the secrets of the veil led to Noah's death?

He found himself wandering the streets, lost in thought, the cityscape around him merely a backdrop to his internal turmoil. Images of Noah's face haunted his waking hours, a constant reminder of the friend he had lost.

"Tim," Georgia's voice brought him back to reality one afternoon as they gathered in his lounge room. Her eyes showed concern, her voice gentle. "You can't blame yourself. What happened was beyond our control."

Tim looked at her wearily. "Was it, Georgia? Was it really beyond our control? We were playing with forces we didn't understand. And now Noah is dead."

Georgia's closest friend was gone, yet her focus was not on the grief but on the strange circumstances of his death. She looked at Tim, her eyes filled with determination. "We have to find out what happened, Tim. For Noah's sake."

Heidi chimed in, "I've been going over the data, the recordings, everything. There's something here, something we're missing. Noah's connection to the veil, the way the equipment reacted... it all means something."

The room was filled with a sense of restless energy, the atmosphere charged with a combination of grief, guilt, confusion, and a burning desire to understand.

They spent hours reading through the data, analysing every aspect of the experiment. The more they delved into the details, the more puzzling it became.

Noah's connection to the veil had been unique, something beyond mere scientific interaction. His descriptions, his insights, the way he had reacted – it all pointed to something profound, something inexplicable.

And yet, the answers eluded them.

Hours turned into days, and the investigation took on a life of its own. The group worked tirelessly, driven by an ongoing need to understand, to make sense of the senseless.

Tim's guilt began to morph into a relentless determination, a single-minded focus on uncovering an explanation. He knew that he owed it to Noah, that the answers were the only way to honour his memory.

Georgia, too, found herself consumed by the mystery, her grief giving way to a fascination with the unknown. She knew that Noah would want her to continue, to follow the trail he had blazed.

And Heidi was drawn deeper and deeper into the complexity of the veil. Her analytical mind was both intrigued and challenged by the phenomena they were studying.

They consulted with experts, sought opinions from colleagues, even reached out to skeptics and critics. They left no stone unturned, no avenue unexplored.

And slowly, pieces of the puzzle began to fall into place. They discovered patterns, connections, subtle nuances that had previously escaped their notice. The veil was not a static phenomenon; it was dynamic, ever-changing, interacting with their world in ways they had never anticipated.

The more they learned, the more they realised how little they truly understood.

And yet, they were undeterred.

They knew that they were on the cusp of something monumental, something that could redefine their understanding of reality itself.

But they also knew that the road ahead was fraught with uncertainty, that the veil's secrets were not easily uncovered.

They were in uncharted territory, facing challenges and obstacles that were both daunting and exhilarating.

But they were united in their purpose, bound together by a shared quest for understanding, a determination to honour Noah's memory by uncovering the secrets he had died trying to understand.

They knew that the answers were within reach, that the veil was calling to them, beckoning them forward.

And they knew that they would not rest, that they would not stop until they had found the answers they sought.

Noah's death had been a tragedy, a shocking and sudden loss that had shaken them to their core.

But it had also been a catalyst, a turning point that had galvanised them, that had given them a renewed sense of purpose and direction.

They were no longer merely researchers, scientists seeking knowledge.

They were explorers, pioneers venturing into the unknown, driven by a passion that transcended mere academic interest.

They were on a journey, a quest for understanding that had become a personal mission, a pursuit that was both a tribute to their lost friend and a testament to their unwavering commitment to the truth.

And they knew that they were not alone, that Noah's spirit was with them, guiding them, urging them forward.

The investigation was far from over.

CHAPTER 5.4: ECHOES OF GUIDANCE

The notes began to appear shortly after Noah's death, subtle at first, but growing in frequency and complexity. Random letters tucked away in unexpected places, text messages from unknown numbers, symbols sketched on their research papers.

Each one was mildly cryptic, leaving room for interpretation, yet undeniably connected to the veil and their investigation. They seemed almost too coincidental to be accidental, too pointed to be mere pranks.

Tim found the first one, a slip of paper tucked inside a book on theoretical physics. It contained a string of numbers and a simple equation. Initially dismissing it as a random scribble, he soon realised that the numbers correlated with specific data from their veil experiments.

Georgia's discovery was more personal. She received a text message one night, the sender's ID hidden. It read: "Seek the rhythm within chaos." It made no sense at the time, but in the coming days, it became a clue, guiding them towards a new understanding of the veil's patterns.

Heidi's experience was the most startling. While working late one night, she found a series of symbols drawn on her workstation, symbols she had discussed with Noah in their early research that nobody else would know about. They pointed to a connection between the veil's activity and specific environmental factors.

Together, they began to piece together the puzzle, each message guiding them, nudging them in new directions. The investigation intensified, fuelled by these mysterious communiqués.

Was there something supernatural at play? Or were they the work of someone else? Or someone trying to prank them?

The question hung in the air, adding intrigue and complexity to their pursuit. Each new discovery seemed to validate the idea that these messages were more than mere coincidence.

They followed the leads, delving deeper into the veil's intricacies. Patterns emerged, connections were made, and slowly, the picture began to form.

They found links between the veil's activity and natural phenomena, correlations with human behaviour and consciousness. The veil was not an isolated occurrence; it was part of a complex web of interconnections, a manifestation of something far more profound.

The messages continued to arrive, each one more precise, more targeted. They led the group to hidden archives, long-forgotten research papers, obscure references in ancient texts.

Each discovery opened new doors, shedding light on aspects of the veil they had never considered, taking them down paths they had never explored.

They travelled to distant libraries, consulted with unconventional thinkers, and even sought the help of a renowned cryptographer, Professor Jacobie Malgrave.

Jacobie was a lean, ageing man, with a sharp mind and an unquenchable thirst for puzzles. He was intrigued by the messages, drawn to their complexity and ambiguity.

"These are not random," he told them, peering at the notes through his thick glasses. "There's a structure here, a hidden logic. Whoever is sending these knows what they are doing."

Working with Jacobie, they began to decode the messages, unravelling their hidden meanings. The process was arduous, requiring patience, intuition, and an uncanny ability to think outside conventional boundaries.

As they delved deeper, they found layers within layers, meanings within meanings. The messages were not merely guiding them; they were teaching them, helping them see the veil in a whole new light.

It was a humbling experience, a realisation that they were part of something much larger, something that transcended mere scientific curiosity. Echoes of guidance from a source they could not identify.

Were they truly from Noah? Was his spirit somehow reaching out to them from beyond the grave? Surely not, that would be such a strange concept, and Tim wasn't sure if he even believed an afterlife existed. Or were they the work of someone else, someone who understood the veil, someone who wanted them to succeed?

The question lingered, a tantalising mystery that added depth and intrigue to their pursuit.

They knew that they were on the brink of something monumental, something that could redefine their understanding of reality itself.

But they also knew that the road ahead was filled with uncertainty, that the answers would not come easily, that the messages were only part of a much larger puzzle.

They were explorers, venturing into unknown territory, guided by echoes of wisdom, driven by a relentless pursuit of understanding.

And they knew that they were not alone, that the veil was calling to them, beckoning them forward, urging them to continue.

The investigation was far from over.

CHAPTER 5.5: OBSESSION AND DOUBT

Tim's eyes were bloodshot, the piercing blue now obscured by an exhaustion that went beyond physical tiredness. The messages—those inexplicable, bewildering messages that appeared out of nowhere—had become his sole focus. Noah's death, those cryptic signs, had lit a fire in him that refused to be extinguished.

The study in his home had turned into a command centre of sorts, the walls adorned with scribbled notes, maps, pictures, and everything that connected to the veil. Strings connected the dots, evidence of his restless pursuit. He'd spend nights there, skipping meals, missing sleep, driven by a force that was as consuming as it was inexplicable.

Georgia and Heidi would often find him hunched over his desk, studying the data, the connections he'd made, the paths he'd pursued. His eyes would be wild with determination, yet tinged with a hint of something more profound, more disturbing.

"What's happened to you, Tim?" Georgia would ask, concern in her eyes. Her voice, once filled with excitement and intrigue, now carried a note of fear. "You're consumed by this. It's not healthy."

But Tim would brush her concerns aside, his mind already racing to the next clue, the next lead. His obsession was not merely about solving a mystery; it had become personal. Noah's death had shaken him to the core, and the messages that seemed to come from beyond had instilled in him a responsibility he could not ignore.

Yet, beneath the obsession, doubts began to gnaw at him. Was he losing his grip on reality? Were his motives pure, or was he driven by something darker, something he did not fully understand?

He'd find himself staring into the mirror, searching for the man he once was, looking for a glimpse of sanity in his own reflection. The face that looked back was unfamiliar, gaunt, and driven by a singular purpose.

"I must know," he'd whisper to himself, his voice cracking. "I must find the answers to this."

He began to question his own ethics, the lines he was willing to cross. In his relentless pursuit, he found himself bending rules, ignoring moral constraints, driven by a need that went beyond rationality.

One night, as he sat alone in his study, the weight of his obsession and the doubts that accompanied it became too much to bear.

He broke down, tears streaming down his face, a mixture of frustration, desperation, and a profound sense of loss.

Why was he doing this? What was driving him? Was he honouring Noah's memory, or was he merely using his death as an excuse to delve into an obsession that had taken over his life?

He was lost, adrift in a sea of questions, doubts, and an obsession that threatened to consume him.

The clock ticked ominously in the background, each second a reminder of the time slipping away, the mystery growing deeper, the obsession growing stronger.

His phone buzzed, breaking the silence. It was a message from Heidi, a new lead, a new direction. Tim wiped his tears and looked at the screen, his heart pounding.

He was back on the trail, the doubts momentarily pushed aside, the obsession once again taking over.

The pursuit of the unknown was a relentless siren's call, and Tim was unable to resist.

He plunged back into the investigation, his soul torn between the need to know and the doubts that continued to plague him.

But the messages, the signs, the connection to something beyond kept pulling him in, a gravitational force that refused to let go.

The questions remained, the doubts lingered, but the obsession was unbreakable.

CHAPTER 5.6: A RELENTLESS PURSUIT

In the following days, Tim's pursuit of the mystery intensified. The messages were coming more frequently, each one a beacon guiding him down a path that twisted and turned but seemed to be leading somewhere significant. Georgia and Heidi, while worried about Tim's obsession, couldn't deny the sense that they were on the brink of a major discovery.

Tim's world had become a whirlwind of research, stakeouts, interviews, and late-night analysis. He was a man possessed, driven by a desire that went beyond mere curiosity. The ethical lines were blurring; he found himself bribing a security guard for access to a restricted area, hacking into a database for confidential files, and confronting people who seemed to hold pieces of the puzzle.

And through it all, it seemed the messages continued to appear. Random words in the articles of old newspapers, noise in the static of a radio broadcast, even imaginary shapes in the patterns of rain on a windowpane. Some were clear, others required interpretation, but all seemed to be guiding them towards something.

His relationship with Georgia and Heidi was strained. They were supportive but concerned. Georgia held a feeling of uncertainty when she looked at Tim, her older brother transformed into something she didn't quite recognise.

"You have to slow down, Tim," Heidi urged one night as they sat in a dimly-lit cafe, going over the latest clues. "You're pushing yourself too hard. You're pushing all of us too hard."

"I can't stop," Tim replied, his voice hoarse from lack of sleep and constant talking. "We're close, I can feel it. Noah is guiding us, I know he is."

But even as he said the words, doubts continued to plague him. Was this really Noah's guidance, or was it all in his mind? Was he leading them to a breakthrough, or down a path of madness?

The more he discovered, the more complex the mystery became. It was like peeling layers from an onion, each one revealing something new, yet hiding something else. The connections were there, but they were elusive, always just out of reach.

And then, just when it seemed like the answers were slipping away, a breakthrough.

A hidden room in an old library, concealed behind a bookshelf, filled with documents, artefacts., and a journal that seemed to hold the key to understanding the veil.

Tim's heart pounded as he leafed through the pages, his hands trembling. The words were a mixture of scientific observations, personal reflections, and something more, something that resonated with Tim's own experience.

He looked up at Georgia and Heidi, his eyes wide with realisation. "We've found it," he whispered, his voice filled with awe and trepidation. "We've found the key to the veil."

But even as they celebrated the discovery, Tim's doubts lingered. The obsession had taken a toll, not just on him, but on those he cared about. The ethical lines had been crossed, the moral compass skewed.

Was it worth it? Was the pursuit of truth more important than the means to achieve it?

As they delved deeper into the newly discovered information, the stakes grew higher, and Tim's internal struggle intensified.

He was on the edge of discovery, on the brink of understanding something that had eluded humanity for centuries.

But at what cost?

The relentless pursuit had brought him to the threshold of the unknown, but the doubts, the questions, the ethical dilemmas remained.

The answers were within reach, but the path was fraught with uncertainty.

Tim stood at the crossroads, torn between the obsession that had consumed him and the doubts that threatened to unravel everything.

The mystery was deepening, the intrigue growing, and Tim's journey was far from over.

His pursuit of the veil had become a reflection of his own inner turmoil, a struggle that would define not just the investigation but the very core of who he was.

The next phase of the journey awaited, the unknown beckoned, and Tim knew that there was no turning back.

The veil was calling, and he was ready to answer.

CHAPTER 5.7: A PURPOSE RENEWED

The room fell into silence as Tim closed the journal, the weight of their discovery settling over them. The dim glow of a desk lamp cast long shadows over the ancient artefacts. and worn documents, giving the hidden room a timeless feel.

"This changes everything," Georgia finally said, breaking the silence. Her voice was low, filled with the gravity of what they'd uncovered.

"It does," Tim agreed, looking up at her, starting to feel traces of an optimism that had been missing for a while.

"But what do we do now?" Heidi asked, her face reflecting the uncertainty they all felt. "We have these clues, these messages, but what do they mean? What are we supposed to do with them?"

Tim stood, his body aching from hours of relentless work but his mind sharper than ever. "We follow them," he said simply. "We follow the clues, the messages, wherever they lead us. We owe it to Noah. We owe it to ourselves."

Georgia and Heidi exchanged glances, uncertainty clear in the room.

"We're in uncharted territory," Georgia said slowly. "We don't know what we're dealing with, what dangers we might face."

"But we can't stop now," Tim replied, his voice filled with conviction. "We've come too far, uncovered too much. We can't turn back."

He paused, looking at each of them, searching for agreement. "We have a chance to understand something that has baffled humanity for generations. We have a chance to honour Noah's memory by finding the answers he died seeking."

The room was quiet again, with Tim's words sinking in.

Finally, Heidi spoke, her voice filled with resolve. "I'm with you. We have to see this through, no matter what."

Georgia nodded, her eyes meeting Tim's, a shared understanding passing between them. "We do it together. We follow the clues, we uncover the truth, and we do it in Noah's memory."

Tim's heart swelled with gratitude and pride. They were united, committed to the pursuit of the truth, no matter where it led.

They spent the rest of the night organising the clues, mapping out a plan, and preparing for the next phase of their journey.

The messages were their guide, a series of cryptic hints and symbols that seemed to be leading them to specific locations, specific people, specific pieces of the puzzle.

The path was unclear, filled with potential danger, but they were driven by a sense of purpose that went beyond mere curiosity.

They were on a quest, a quest to uncover the secrets of the veil, to understand the unknown, to honour the memory of a friend.

As the first light of dawn began to filter through the cracks in the old library's windows, they finally called it a night.

They stood together, looking at the maps and notes spread out before them, a sense of anticipation and trepidation in the air.

"We will do this," Georgia said quietly. "For Noah."

They left the hidden room, locking the door behind them, the weight of their discovery and the responsibility of their quest settling over them.

As they stepped out into the cool morning air, a sense of foreboding hung in the air, a hint of the challenges and mysteries that awaited them.

But they were ready. They were united. They were driven.

The next phase of their journey was about to begin, and they were prepared to face it head-on.

The veil was calling, and they were answering. The pursuit of the truth had become more than an investigation; it had become a mission.

A mission to uncover the secrets of the unknown, to honour the memory of a lost friend, to seek answers to questions that had haunted humanity for generations. With a sense of renewed purpose and a hint of foreboding, they set out, ready to face whatever lay ahead.

CHAPTER 6.1: UNRAVELLING THE TRAIL

Melbourne's historical district was quiet at this time of night, the streets nearly deserted, but Tim's heart was racing as they approached the site indicated by the first clue. An old church, built centuries ago, stood as a silent guardian of secrets long forgotten. This was not a place they had expected their investigation to lead, but the messages were clear, the cryptic notes pointing to this very location.

"He said the answers lie in history's embrace," Tim whispered, recalling the words from one of the mysterious messages they had received. "This church is one of the oldest buildings in the city. There must be something here."

Georgia was fixed on watching the towering steeple, her mind working furiously. "It could be something hidden within the architecture, a document, or a symbol that has been overlooked."

The trio made their way carefully to the entrance, the old wooden door creaking ominously as they pushed it open. Inside, the dimly lit interior was filled with the smell of aged wood and the lingering scent of incense. Shadows danced on the walls as their flashlights cut through the darkness.

Heidi was the first to spot something. "Look here," she said, her voice hushed with excitement as she pointed to an almost invisible carving on one of the pews. It was a symbol, intricate and delicate, and yet something about it seemed familiar.

"That's the same symbol we found in Noah's notes," Tim said, recognising it instantly. "It's part of the pattern he was trying to decipher."

The realisation that they were on the right track filled them with a renewed sense of purpose. They continued to search the church, uncovering more symbols, hidden inscriptions, and concealed compartments.

Each discovery brought them closer to understanding the veil, the secrets it held, and the forces that had conspired to keep it hidden. The more they uncovered, the more they realised how complex and far-reaching the mystery was.

The trail led them from the main hall of the church downstairs to a hidden chamber, where they found documents dating back centuries. Written in ancient Greek, these texts held keys to unlocking the puzzle. Georgia, a current university student of ancient languages, painstakingly translated them, revealing fragments of information that connected the dots.

"This is incredible," Georgia said, her voice trembling with excitement as she read from one of the documents. "It speaks of a secret society called The Midnight Order, a group that has been guarding the secrets of the veil for generations. They've been here, watching, guarding, ensuring that the secrets remain hidden."

They continued to follow the trail, the messages guiding them to overlooked witnesses, individuals who had seen or experienced something related to the veil but had been dismissed or silenced.

One witness, an old librarian named Mrs. Simmons, spoke of strange occurrences, unexplained phenomena that had haunted her for years. Her testimony provided a vital piece of the puzzle, confirming their suspicions and opening new avenues of investigation.

The momentum continued to build as they unravelled the trail. The messages, believed to be from Noah, were leading them down a path filled with intrigue, danger, and revelation.

Each clue, each discovery was a step closer to understanding the veil, a step closer to uncovering the truth that had eluded them for so long.

But as they delved deeper, they began to realise that they were not alone. The shadows were moving, unseen eyes were watching, and the danger was growing.

The Midnight Order were aware of their pursuit, and they were not going to give up their secrets easily.

As Tim, Georgia, and Heidi stood in the hidden chamber, pouring over the documents and piecing together the puzzle, they knew that they were on the brink of something extraordinary.

But they also knew that they were playing a dangerous game, a game that could cost them everything.

The trail was unravelling, the pieces were falling into place, and the mystery was beginning to reveal itself.

But the stakes were high, the danger was real, and the journey was far from over.

CHAPTER 6.2: UNRAVELLING SECRETS

As Georgia fiddled with the radio controls in their rented van, the crackling voice of a late-night talk show host melded with the distant howls of the wind. She, Tim, and Heidi were deep into the night, driving to the coordinates inscribed in one of the enigmatic messages. Their path had been riddled with hidden documents, secret locations, and overlooked witnesses, and now they were being led to the heart of The Midnight Order's headquarters.

"So, The Midnight Order," Heidi broke the silence, her voice tinged with disbelief. "It sounds like a group of kids playing at being detectives, not a shadowy organisation."

Tim's hands clenched the steering wheel. "It's no child's play, Heidi. The evidence suggests that they've been guarding, or maybe even controlling, this veil thing for centuries."

Georgia's heart pounded as she considered the gravity of the situation. "We've gotten further than anyone else. What if they're watching us? What if they know we're onto them?"

Tim's face was stern, his determination evident. "Then we must be even more careful. We owe it to Noah."

The clues had led them throughout Melbourne, through ancient libraries, derelict buildings, and to the doorsteps of people who seemed to have been waiting for someone to ask the right questions. Each step was like a piece of a vast puzzle, clicking into place, forming a picture that was both fascinating and terrifying.

The Midnight Order's hidden documents painted a picture of control, manipulation, and power that reached into the highest echelons of governments and corporations. Their influence was profound, their secrets guarded with a ferocity that chilled the bones.

Now, as they approached the location indicated by the final clue, they knew they were at the threshold of something immense. The GPS led them down a twisting road, the dark forest around them pressing in like the watching eyes of unseen sentinels.

"Here," Tim said, slowing the van to a stop near a hidden trail.

They got out, flashlights in hand, and followed a well-worn path. It led them to a cavernous opening, a chamber hidden within the earth itself.

"This is it," Georgia whispered, her excitement mixed with fear. "Whatever we find here, it's the key. I can feel it."

The walls of the cavern were covered in ancient symbols and drawings, some of which they recognised from The Midnight Order's documents. Tim took a careful look at a wall inscribed with a cryptic code.

"It's a timeline," he realised, tracing the lines with his fingers. "A history of The Midnight Order's actions and decisions."

Heidi's attention was caught by a series of pictures depicting what looked like the veil itself. "This... this might explain what it is, what it does."

They delved deeper, the chamber's secrets unravelling before them, the legacy of The Midnight Order laid bare. It was a treasure trove of information, a direct line to understanding the mysterious force they'd been pursuing.

As dawn approached, the realisation dawned on them that they had found the breakthrough they needed. They were on the verge of uncovering truths that had been hidden for centuries.

With a renewed sense of purpose and a hint of foreboding, they knew their journey was far from over. The Midnight Order's secrets were now theirs to unravel, and the veil was within their grasp.

But as they left the chamber, a shadow flickered in the corner of Georgia's vision, a fleeting sense that they were not alone. The secrets they had uncovered were protected for a reason, and the guardians of those secrets were undoubtedly watching.

CHAPTER 6.3: BRIDGING REALMS

As the days turned into weeks, their tireless efforts began to illuminate the shadowy edges of the puzzle. The labyrinth they had once perceived was no longer insurmountable. Tim, engrossed in countless ancient documents and high-tech data, found himself in a whirlwind of scientific explanations and ancient wisdom.

Scrawled diagrams, esoteric symbols, and lines of code filled papers strewn across Tim's study, bearing testament to their relentless pursuit.

Each day Tim dove into this ocean of knowledge. And each day, he surfaced with pearls of understanding that started to form a coherent explanation. A statement that attempted to grasp the concept of the veil. It was like observing an elusive creature that lurked beneath the water surface, its form flickering, fragmented by ripples. But with every passing day, the image became more precise, more comprehensive.

He discovered scientific theories that suggested the existence of a multi-dimensional reality. Physics at the quantum level spoke of particles existing in two places simultaneously, of entanglement where the state of one particle could influence another instantaneously over vast distances. Tim began to see parallels between these theories and the ancient wisdom documented by The Midnight Order.

The veil, he theorised, could be a tangible manifestation of these theories—a layer of reality that existed alongside ours, but was usually obscured, visible only under certain circumstances. It wasn't magic, nor was it purely scientific. It was a phenomenon that straddled the line between the physical and the metaphysical, a reality at the intersection of science, philosophy, and spirituality.

"This is groundbreaking," Heidi remarked one day, reading through Tim's notes, her eyebrows knitted in concentration. "If this is correct, it means our understanding of reality is fundamentally flawed."

Tim nodded. "And it means we might be closer to understanding what happened to Noah. To understanding the message he's trying to send."

Despite their groundbreaking discoveries, their investigation was not without obstacles. There still pieces missing, elements that didn't quite fit. Each step forward seemed to be accompanied by more questions, and every answer hinted at a more significant, more complicated puzzle. But despite this, the thread of understanding was beginning to weave a tapestry of meaning that brought them closer to the veil than they'd ever been before.

CHAPTER 6.4: UNVEILING SECRETS

Georgia sat on the floor, a sea of ancient texts surrounding her, her thoughts consumed by the abstract ideas that danced before her eyes. The Midnight Order's cryptic writings spoke in poetic, symbolic language, but there was a practicality behind the mysticism, a science behind the spirituality.

The veil, she realised, was not just a metaphor or a mere concept. It was a living, breathing entity that resonated with human consciousness. It was as if human thought and emotion were keys that could unlock the doors to other realms, connecting the finite to the infinite.

She found herself drawn to one document in particular, its pages worn and weathered, the ink faded. It was an original manuscript from The Midnight Order, written by one of its ancient scholars. Here, the veil was described as the "threshold of the known and unknown, where our realm meets the boundless soul."

She shared her findings with Tim and Heidi, her voice filled with excitement. "This isn't just a discovery for the scientific community. This is something that challenges our very understanding of existence. It suggests that our connection to the universe is more profound than we ever realised."

Tim, equally captivated by the findings, started to map out the connections between the scientific theories and the ancient writings, noting how they complemented each other. The metaphysical principles of The Midnight Order were not in conflict with modern science but seemed to fill the gaps, adding layers of complexity and richness.

Together, the group started to synthesise their findings into a cohesive whole. They integrated the cryptic messages they believed to be from Noah with the scientific data and the wisdom of The Midnight Order.

Slowly, the outline of a truth began to form, one that was both new and ancient, that spanned the boundaries of conventional understanding. The veil was not just a phenomenon; it was a testament to the interconnectedness of all things.

They felt the weight of the responsibility on their shoulders. They were no longer just researchers or investigators; they were the bearers of a revelation that could change the way humanity perceived reality.

The challenge now was to communicate this understanding to the world, to translate it into a language that could be comprehended, digested, and appreciated by others.

They knew that their journey was far from over. But they also knew that they had uncovered something extraordinary, something that transcended conventional wisdom and opened the door to a new frontier of understanding.

Their resolve was strengthened, their purpose clarified. They would bring the knowledge of the veil to the world, honouring Noah's memory, guided by the clues he had left behind, driven by the belief that they were part of something much larger than themselves.

With a renewed sense of determination and a hint of foreboding, they closed the chapter on their investigation, ready to embark on the next phase of their extraordinary journey.

CHAPTER 6.5: THE GATEWAY

As the clues unravelled and the pieces of the puzzle fell into place, Tim, Georgia, and Heidi found themselves at the brink of an extraordinary revelation. The veil, which had once seemed an abstract idea, a mere scientific anomaly, was emerging as something far greater, something deeply connected to the human experience.

In the office of Dr. Xavier Harlow, a renowned physicist who had shown interest in their findings, they began to share their discoveries, carefully balancing the scientific, philosophical, and spiritual aspects.

"The veil, as we understand it, is not a mere distortion of reality or a random occurrence. It's more of a gateway," Tim began, his voice filled with both awe and excitement. "A gateway that bridges the physical world with something deeper, something beyond our conventional understanding."

Dr. Xavier Harlow, a man of analytical mind and skeptical disposition, listened intently, his eyebrows furrowing as he considered the implications. "You're suggesting that it's a phenomenon that transcends the physical realm? That's a bold claim."

"Yes," Georgia replied, taking over from Tim. "But it's more than a claim. We've found evidence in both ancient wisdom and modern science that points to the existence of a connection between the human consciousness and this...this threshold."

"The Midnight Order," Heidi added, referring to the secret society whose writings had offered profound insights, "believed the veil to be a living entity, a protector, and a teacher. They saw it as a link between the human soul and the cosmos."

Xavier's face showed signs of both fascination and skepticism. The idea was revolutionary, unorthodox, and challenged the very foundations of conventional science.

"Imagine," Tim continued, his voice filled with passion, "a world where the barrier between the seen and unseen is not as rigid as we thought. Where there's an interaction between the mind and the universe at a level we're only beginning to comprehend. The veil could be a means of communication, a tool for growth, a pathway to enlightenment."

The room fell into a thoughtful silence as the weight of these words settled upon them. The veil was no longer just an academic interest or a scientific curiosity; it was a revelation that could redefine the way they understood existence.

But with this realisation came challenges and responsibilities. How would they present these findings to a world unprepared for such a radical shift in understanding? How would they navigate the skepticism, the disbelief, the potential backlash?

The significance of the veil was profound, its implications far-reaching. It opened doors to new possibilities, new ways of thinking, new horizons of human potential.

Yet, it also raised questions, doubts, and uncertainties. Was humanity ready for such a revelation? Were they, as the bearers of this knowledge, prepared for the path that lay ahead?

The journey had only just begun, and as they stood at the brink of a new frontier, they knew that they were venturing into uncharted territory, guided by a blend of faith, reason, and intuition.

Their exploration of the veil was taking them not only into the depths of the cosmos but into the very core of human existence. It was a journey of discovery, reflection, and transformation, and it was a journey they were committed to undertaking, no matter where it might lead.

The veil was no longer a distant, abstract concept; it was a part of them, a reflection of their own complexity, their own potential, their own humanity. It was a gateway to a new understanding, a new way of living, a new era of human evolution.

And they were the pioneers, the explorers, the torchbearers of this new world.

CHAPTER 6.6: THE NEW UNDERSTANDING

Tim, Georgia, and Heidi sat around a worn wooden table, their minds reeling from the magnitude of their discoveries. The veil had become a living metaphor, a symbol of a journey that transcended the boundaries of time, space, and understanding.

Each of them felt a profound connection to the veil, a resonance that went beyond mere intellectual curiosity. It was as if they were being drawn into a dance with the universe, a dance that was both thrilling and terrifying.

Dr. Xavier Harlow's skepticism had given way to genuine interest, and he had provided them access to his vast library of scientific and philosophical texts. The old books, manuscripts, and journals were like keys to a door they were just beginning to unlock.

As they delved into the purpose and nature of the veil, they discovered threads of thought that connected different cultures, different epochs, different disciplines. From the mystics of the East to the scientists of the West, from the ancient sages to contemporary philosophers, the concept of a gateway or threshold had been explored, studied, and revered.

The veil was not just a scientific anomaly; it was a universal concept, a shared understanding, a bridge that connected humanity to something greater, something divine.

"It's as if the veil is a mirror," Georgia said, her voice filled with wonder. "A mirror that reflects our own consciousness, our own longing for understanding, our own search for meaning."

"It's more than that," Heidi added, her mind racing with insights. "It's a teacher, a guide, a protector. It challenges us to grow, to evolve, to become more than we are. It invites us into a dialogue with the cosmos, a conversation that goes beyond words, beyond thoughts, beyond beliefs."

Tim's eyes were filled with a fire of determination as he listened to his friends. The veil was not just a personal journey; it was a collective one. It was a call to humanity, a call to awaken, to recognise. the interconnectedness of all life, the sacredness of existence.

"The Midnight Order was not just a secret society," Tim said, his voice filled with conviction. "They were visionaries, pioneers, seekers of truth. They understood the significance of the veil, its role as a bridge between worlds, its potential to transform humanity."

The room was filled with a sense of awe, a sense of purpose, a sense of destiny. They were not just investigators; they were messengers, bearers of a truth that could change the world.

But with this realisation came a sense of responsibility, a sense of duty. How would they share this discovery? How would they navigate the skepticism, the ridicule, the fear that might arise?

They were venturing into unknown territory, walking a path that was both ancient and new, both familiar and foreign. They were explorers of the mind, the heart, the soul.

The veil was not just a scientific phenomenon; it was a spiritual one. It was not just a mystery to be solved; it was a wisdom to be embraced.

It was a reminder of the interconnectedness of all things, the unity of all life, the oneness of existence. It was a call to recognise. the divinity within, the sacredness without.

As they sat around that old wooden table, their minds expanded, their hearts opened, their souls stirred, they knew that they were part of something greater, something grander, something divine.

CHAPTER 6.7: A SHATTERING REVELATION

The days that followed were a whirlwind of activity for Tim, Georgia, and Heidi. Their understanding of the veil was growing exponentially, each discovery leading to another, each insight opening up new vistas of thought. The convergence of science, philosophy, and spirituality was thrilling, but it was also daunting. They were probing into realms that few had ventured into before, navigating a complex web of ideas and implications.

Dr. Xavier Harlow was a constant presence, both a mentor and a collaborator, guiding them, challenging them, encouraging them. His experience and wisdom were invaluable, his skepticism tempered by a genuine fascination with the phenomenon they were exploring.

The research was intense and demanding, the hours long and gruelling. But there was an excitement in the air, a sense of momentum, a feeling that they were on the verge of something extraordinary.

Tim was the most relentless, his mind racing with theories and hypotheses, his passion for understanding driving him forward. He was like a man possessed, his connection to the veil personal, his commitment to its exploration unwavering.

It was late one night when it happened. Tim was alone in the library, surrounded by stacks of books and piles of papers, his eyes bleary, his mind weary. He was reviewing an ancient manuscript, a treatise on the nature of reality written by a philosopher of The Midnight Order.

As he read, something caught his eye, a phrase, a sentence, a passage that seemed oddly familiar. He looked closer, his mind suddenly alert, his intuition tingling. There was something here, something important, something profound.

He began to cross-reference, to compare, to analyse. He pulled out other texts, other documents, other writings of The Midnight Order. He felt that he was on to something, something big, something that could change everything.

Hours turned into more hours, the night slipping away, the dawn approaching. He was so close, so very close. He could feel it, taste it, almost touch it. It was right there, right in front of him, waiting to be discovered.

And then it hit him, like a bolt of lightning, like a thunderclap, like a seismic shock that reverberated through his entire being.

He found it. He understood it. He saw it.

The revelation was shattering, earth-shattering, mind-shattering. It was so simple, yet so complex, so obvious, yet so obscure. It was a paradox, a contradiction, a conundrum.

He could barely breathe, his heart pounding, his hands shaking. This was it, the answer, the key, the breakthrough.

He grabbed his phone, dialling Georgia, his voice urgent, his words tumbling out.

"Georgia, it's Tim. I've found something. Something big. Something that changes everything. You need to come. Now."

There was no time to explain, no time to elaborate. The urgency was palpable, the excitement contagious.

Georgia and Heidi arrived within the hour, their faces etched with curiosity, their eyes wide with anticipation.

"What is it, Tim?" Georgia asked, her voice tinged with excitement. "What have you found?"

Tim looked at them, his face pale, his eyes blazing with a fire of discovery. "It's the veil," he said, his voice almost a whisper. "It's not what we thought. It's not what anyone thought. It's... it's something else."

He paused, his mind grappling with the enormity of what he had uncovered, the implications staggering, the ramifications profound.

"It's a message," he finally said, his voice breaking with emotion. "A message from the past. For us. For humanity."

Georgia and Heidi exchanged a glance, their faces reflecting a mixture of confusion and intrigue.

"What do you mean, a message?" Heidi asked, her voice filled with skepticism. "What kind of message? From whom? For what purpose?"

Tim took a deep breath, his mind still reeling, his thoughts still jumbled.

"It's a code," he said, his voice filled with conviction. "A code embedded in the fabric of reality. A code that has been waiting to be deciphered, to be understood, to be revealed."

He paused again, his eyes searching theirs, his words weighted with significance.

"It's a warning," he finally said, his voice sombre, his face grave. "A warning of something coming. Something big. Something that could change everything. Forever."

The room fell silent, the words hanging in the air, the magnitude of the revelation sinking in.

A warning? A code? A message? What did it all mean? What were they supposed to do?

The chapter ended with a sense of foreboding, a sense of uncertainty, a sense of destiny.

They had uncovered something extraordinary, something unprecedented, something that could alter the course of human history.

And they were the ones chosen to decipher it, to understand it, to act upon it.

CHAPTER 6.8: THE WEIGHT OF DISCOVERY

The following days were filled with an urgency that none of them had ever felt before. The revelation that Tim had uncovered was not merely an intellectual curiosity; it bore implications that were deeply serious and far-reaching. The veil's warning, whatever it was, demanded their full attention.

They were no longer just researchers probing into an unknown phenomenon. They were now the bearers of a secret that might hold the key to something monumental.

Tim led the way, his mind a whirlpool of activity, driven by a need to understand fully what the code within the veil was trying to convey. The message, if indeed it was a message, was complex and multifaceted, a puzzle within a puzzle, a riddle wrapped in an enigma.

Georgia and Heidi were equally consumed, their skills and expertise pushed to the limits as they delved into the arcane, the esoteric, the profound. Dr. Harlow, too, was drawn into the vortex, his skepticism replaced by a growing sense of awe and wonder.

Days turned into nights, and nights turned into days, as they probed deeper and deeper into the mystery. The library became their sanctuary, their laboratory, their battleground. Books were strewn everywhere, papers scattered, computers humming, minds working.

They delved into physics, exploring theories of reality that defied conventional understanding. They studied ancient philosophies, seeking wisdom that transcended time and space. They consulted obscure texts, reaching out to scholars and experts, following leads that took them down unexpected paths.

They were like detectives, hunting for clues, piecing together evidence, building a case. The code was elusive, its meaning hidden, its message cryptic. But they were determined, relentless, unyielding. They would not be denied; they would not be defeated.

The more they learned, the more they realised how little they knew. The veil was not just a scientific anomaly; it was a philosophical conundrum, a spiritual enigma, a metaphysical puzzle. It defied categorisation, transcended definition, resisted explanation.

It was a gateway, yes, but to what? It was a protector, perhaps, but of what? It was a teacher, certainly, but of what?

They grappled with concepts that were abstract and intangible, ideas that were profound and transcendent. They struggled with questions that were existential and ontological, issues that were ethical and moral.

What was the nature of existence? What was the purpose of life? What was the meaning of being? What was the essence of humanity? What was the role of consciousness? What was the relationship between the individual and the universal? What was the connection between the temporal and the eternal?

They were not just probing into the nature of the veil; they were probing into the nature of reality itself. They were not just seeking to understand a phenomenon; they were seeking to understand existence itself.

And through it all, there was the weight of the warning, the burden of the responsibility, the gravity of the discovery.

What was the warning about? What was it trying to convey? What were they supposed to do?

They felt a sense of destiny, a sense of calling, a sense of purpose. They were not just scholars; they were seekers. They were not just researchers; they were explorers. They were not just academics; they were adventurers.

They were rewriting history, redefining reality, reshaping humanity. And they were doing it together, united by a shared vision, bonded by a common goal, driven by a collective passion.

They would honour Noah's memory. They would fulfil their destiny. They would embrace their purpose. Whatever it took, whatever the cost, whatever the sacrifice.

CHAPTER 7.1: STRATEGY AGAINST SHADOWS

The atmosphere in their makeshift base of operations was palpable with tension. Tim, Georgia, and Heidi sat around the table strewn with maps, historical documents, and pieces of a complex puzzle that was slowly taking shape. In the silence, the enormity of what they were about to undertake began to sink in. They were planning a confrontation with The Midnight Order, an organisation. that had remained hidden in the shadows for centuries. An organisation. that wielded power and influence that stretched far beyond what they had ever imagined.

Tim broke the silence, his voice filled with resolve. "We've uncovered the secret that The Midnight Order wanted to remain hidden. The veil is more than a phenomenon; it's a key to something they've been guarding. We know they're watching us, so we have to be cautious."

Georgia looked at him, her eyes filled with determination but also worry. "We need a plan, Tim. We need to know exactly what we're up against and how we can expose them."

Heidi chimed in, her voice steady. "We need evidence, concrete evidence that can't be refuted. We have to be ready for anything they throw at us."

The next days were a whirlwind of planning, strategizing, and preparing. The trio knew that they were in a race against time. The Midnight Order was undoubtedly aware of their investigations, and it was only a matter of time before they acted.

They divided their tasks, playing to their strengths. Tim focused on understanding the scientific and historical aspects of the veil, tying it into The Midnight Order's interests. Georgia worked on gathering evidence, reaching out to contacts, and piecing together the organisation's movements and operations. Heidi delved into legal aspects, ensuring that they had all the necessary legal grounds to expose The Midnight Order's activities.

The process was arduous, filled with uncertainty and risks. They had to navigate through a web of secrecy, deceit, and danger. They were dealing with an organisation. that had perfected the art of remaining hidden, an organisation. that would stop at nothing to protect its secrets.

They reached out to trusted contacts, seeking assistance and information. They poured over documents, maps, and files, connecting dots and drawing lines. They prepared for contingencies, knowing that they would face obstacles and challenges.

The Midnight Order's reach was vast, its connections deep. They discovered that it had infiltrated various levels of governments, corporations, and institutions. It controlled information, influenced decisions, and manipulated outcomes.

The more they dug, the more they realised the depth of The Midnight Order's control. It was not just about protecting a secret; it was about controlling knowledge, power, and destiny.

They found connections to historical events, patterns that pointed to The Midnight Order's involvement in shaping the course of history. They uncovered links to influential figures, evidence of manipulation and control.

They were uncovering a conspiracy that went beyond anything they had ever imagined. A conspiracy that was interwoven with the fabric of society, politics, and history.

They became more cautious, more aware of the risks. They knew that they were being watched, that their movements were being tracked. They implemented security measures, ensured privacy, and maintained vigilance.

They knew that the confrontation with The Midnight Order was inevitable. They knew that they were up against formidable forces. They knew that they were risking not just their lives but the truth they were trying to expose.

But they were ready. They were prepared. They were determined. They were fighting to expose The Midnight Order, to reveal the truth about the veil, to uncover the secrets that had remained hidden for centuries.

The Midnight Order's time of hiding was over.

CHAPTER 7.2: UNVEILING THE BATTLE

Weeks turned into days, and the urgency grew as the planned confrontation with The Midnight Order approached. Tim, Georgia, and Heidi continued their meticulous planning, leaving no stone unturned. They knew that one misstep could be literally fatal, as was the unfortunate case with Noah, and the line between success and failure was precariously thin.

As Georgia was digging deeper into The Midnight Order's operations, she stumbled upon a hidden server that held sensitive information. It was clear that someone within the organisation. had been watching them. She found detailed reports on their movements, emails they had sent, and even transcripts of conversations they thought were private. It was unsettling, to say the least.

"We've been compromised," Georgia said, her voice trembling as she looked at Tim and Heidi. "They know about our plans. They've been tracking us all along."

Tim hurried over to look at her screen. "Show me."

She guided him through a series of documents, pointing out the connections and the threads that she had uncovered. The realisation settled like a heavy weight, adding yet another layer of complexity to their plan.

Tim stared at the screen in disbelief, absorbing the extent of the infiltration. "This changes everything. They've anticipated our moves. Our strategies, our contacts, everything is exposed."

"They've been playing us," Heidi added, her eyes narrowing. "But how? How did they infiltrate our communications?"

Georgia continued to investigate, uncovering evidence that their secure communication channels had been breached. Sophisticated hacking techniques had been employed to intercept their messages, and it seemed as if a mole within their network had been feeding information back to The Midnight Order.

The realisation was chilling. They were up against an opponent who was not only powerful but highly intelligent and resourceful. The Midnight Order had eyes and ears everywhere, and they had been one step ahead all along.

The trio immediately went into damage control mode. They changed their communication protocols, employing even more secure encryption methods. They reached out to their contacts, warning them about the possible breach and tightening their security measures.

They also re-evaluated their plans, recognising that they had to be more unpredictable. The original strategy to confront The Midnight Order was now too risky; they had to come up with something new, something that would catch them off guard.

"We need to think outside the box," Tim said, his mind racing. "We need to do something they won't expect, something they can't predict."

They brainstormed late into the night, discarding old plans and devising new ones. They incorporated misdirection, creating decoys to confuse their opponents. They developed contingency plans, preparing for every possible scenario. They reached out to unexpected allies, forging new connections that could provide them with an advantage.

It was a race against time, a battle of wits, a game of chess with the highest stakes.

The Midnight Order had shown their hand, revealing their capabilities and their intent. But Tim, Georgia, and Heidi were not defeated. They were determined, resilient, and creative. They had come too far to be stopped, and they had too much to lose to give up.

The revelation that the secret organisation had been monitoring them was a shock, but it was also a wake-up call. It sharpened their focus, heightened their awareness, and strengthened their resolve.

The confrontation was coming, and they were ready. The Midnight Order may have known their plans, but they did not know their spirit, their ingenuity, or their determination.

The day of the confrontation drew near, and the tension was almost unbearable. They reviewed their plan, going over every detail, ensuring that they had considered every possibility. They were prepared for anything, ready to face The Midnight Order head-on.

They knew that they were risking everything. They knew that they were going up against powerful forces. But they also knew that they were fighting for something greater than themselves. They were fighting for truth, for justice, for humanity.

The night before the confrontation, they gathered around the table, looking at each other with a mixture of determination and uncertainty. They were on the cusp of something momentous, something that could change everything.

"We've come so far," Tim said, his voice filled with conviction. "We've uncovered the truth, and now it's time to expose it. We know what we're up against, and we know what we have to do. We're ready."

Georgia reached out, placing her hand on Tim's. "We're in this together. We'll face The Midnight Order, and we'll bring them down. We'll reveal the truth about the veil, and we'll change the world."

Heidi nodded, her eyes reflecting the shared resolve. "We've prepared for this moment. We know what we're doing, and we know why we're doing it. We're fighting for something that matters, something that's bigger than all of us. We'll succeed, and we'll make a difference."

They sat in silence for a moment, each lost in thought, contemplating the significance of what lay ahead.

They were about to confront The Midnight Order, an organisation. that had remained hidden for centuries. They were about to expose the truth about the veil, a truth that could reshape human understanding. They were about to embark on a journey that could change the course of history.

And they were doing it together, united by a common purpose, driven by a shared vision, and guided by a collective mission.

The battle was about to begin, and they were ready.

CHAPTER 7.3: BETRAYED

The trio were concerned. Confused. How did The Midnight Order know so much about their plans? It played in all of their minds over and over. Tim's fingers flew over the keyboard as he accessed a hidden file he had found on his computer, his heart pounding in his chest. It was protected with a password. But Georgia was already working on it, her mind sharp and focused.

"What do you think this file is?" Heidi asked, her voice filled with anticipation.

"It could be anything," Tim replied. "But it's locked for a reason. It must be something important."

Finally, Georgia cracked the password, and the file opened to reveal a series of communications. Emails, texts, transcripts of phone calls. They all pointed to one person: Dr. Xavier Harlow.

The trio's eyes widened as they read the contents, their disbelief growing with every word. Dr. Harlow had been feeding information to The Midnight Order all along. He was one of them.

"It can't be," Heidi whispered, her voice trembling. "Not Dr. Harlow. He was on our side."

"Was he?" Georgia's voice was cold, her eyes fixed on the screen. "Or was he just pretending to be?"

They delved deeper into the evidence, uncovering a trail of deception that led them to the shocking truth. Xavier was a high-ranking member of The Midnight Order, a key player in their operations.

"He's been playing us," Tim said, his voice filled with anger. "He's been manipulating us all along, using us for his own purposes."

In discussion of disbelief, none of the trio noticed the mouse cursor moving across the screen. They were unaware that Xavier was secretly remotely connected to their computer. He knew they had found out that he was the leak.

The betrayal cut deep. Xavier had been a trusted friend, a mentor, a guide. He had helped them, advised them, supported them. And all the while, he had been working against them, undermining their efforts, sabotaging their plans.

"How could he?" Heidi's voice broke, tears welling in her eyes. "How could he betray us like this?"

"We have to confront him," Georgia said, her voice firm. "We have to find out what he knows, what he's done, and why."

They planned their next move carefully, aware that they were treading on dangerous ground. Confronting Dr. Harlow would not be easy. He was cunning, manipulative, and powerful. But they had no choice. They wanted to know the truth.

They tried to contact Dr. Harlow, but he was unreachable. His office was empty, his phone disconnected, his home abandoned. It was as if he had vanished into thin air. They searched for clues, followed leads, and reached out to contacts, but Dr. Harlow was elusive, a ghost who had slipped through their fingers.

Dr. Harlow's betrayal was a wound that cut deep, but it was also a revelation that sharpened their focus.

The battle was far from over, and they were ready to face it, together. They would not stop, not rest, until they had found Dr. Harlow and exposed The Midnight Order for what it truly was. The game of cat and mouse had begun, and they were ready to play.

CHAPTER 7.4: UNRAVELLING SECRETS

The days that followed were a blur of research, analysis, and relentless pursuit. Tim, Georgia, and Heidi were a team possessed, driven by a determination to uncover the hidden agendas of The Midnight Order and the startling secrets they had so artfully concealed. The veil's nature, once an obscure concept, was now an intricate puzzle they were on the brink of solving.

Georgia's background in history led them to archives and ancient manuscripts, where they unearthed documents that spoke of the veil as a phenomenon known to the scholars of old. It was not merely a mysterious occurrence; it was a key to understanding something much greater, something that transcended the boundaries of human knowledge.

In a hidden chamber beneath the city's oldest library, they stumbled upon a collection of correspondences, hidden away for centuries. They were letters between members of a society that had long ago sought to understand the veil.

The messages revealed a group dedicated to the pursuit of understanding, a group that had encountered fierce opposition from powerful forces that saw the veil's nature as a threat.

The more they dug, the more they realised that The Midnight Order's reach was far and wide. Its tentacles extended into the upper echelons of society, influencing governments, controlling media, and even infiltrating scientific communities. This was no small organisation.; it was a vast and powerful network, working behind the scenes to control information, manipulate perceptions, and guide the course of human understanding.

Heidi, who had studied units of psychology at university, helped them understand the mindset of their adversaries. She delved into the psyche of The Midnight Order's members, uncovering a common thread: fear. Fear of change, fear of the unknown, fear of losing control. The veil was a symbol of all that they feared, a challenge to their worldview, a threat to their power.

"What are they so afraid of?" Heidi asked, her voice filled with frustration. "Why go to such lengths to suppress something that could change the way we see the world?"

"Because change is terrifying to those who hold power," Tim replied, his voice tinged with bitterness. "The veil represents a shift, a disruption to the status quo. And they will do anything to prevent that."

The confrontation was no longer just about Dr. Harlow or their personal betrayal. It was about a battle for understanding, a struggle against forces that sought to keep humanity in the dark.

The stakes were high, and the more they learned, the more they realised that this was not a fight they could afford to lose.

"We have to expose them," Georgia said, her eyes shining with determination. "We have to show the world what they've been hiding, what they've been suppressing. We have to bring the truth to light."

But the truth was elusive, and The Midnight Order was a formidable opponent. They had resources, connections, and a willingness to go to great lengths to protect their secrets.

The trio was not deterred. They were united, resolute, and driven by a passion for discovery that could not be extinguished.

They were on a path, a path that would lead them to a confrontation they could not avoid, a showdown that would change everything.

The battle lines were drawn, the players were in place, and the game was afoot. The pursuit of understanding had become a fight for survival, and they were ready to face it, head-on.

As they prepared for the inevitable clash, they knew that they were not just fighting for themselves; they were fighting for something much bigger. They were fighting for knowledge, for enlightenment, for the future of humanity.

The storm was coming.

CHAPTER 7.5: THE UPPER BALLROOM

The headquarters of The Midnight Order was not in some distant castle or hidden underground lair; it was right in the heart of the city, tucked away in the upper ballroom of Flinders Street Station. A location so ordinary, so mundane, it was almost laughable. But it was precisely this ordinariness that made it the perfect hiding place. It made perfect sense why there was such an intense feeling in the trio's previous attendance.

Tim, Georgia, and Heidi carefully planned their approach, going over every detail, leaving nothing to chance. Their hearts pounded with anticipation, nerves tingled with excitement and fear.

"We have one shot at this," Tim said, his voice steady but his eyes masking a hint of anxiety. "We know what they're capable of. We have to be smarter, more strategic. We can't afford to make mistakes."

Georgia nodded, her mind racing with possibilities. "We've come so far, uncovered so much. This is our chance to expose them, to bring everything into the light."

"The upper ballroom," Heidi mused. "It's the perfect place for them to hide. Right under everyone's noses, and yet, who would ever think to look there?"

Under the cover of night, they made their way to Flinders Street Station, the iconic building a symbol of the city's history and culture. Little did the public know what was hidden in its upper reaches.

They entered stealthily, moving through the shadows, avoiding detection. They knew that The Midnight Order was watching, always watching. But they were ready.

As they reached the upper ballroom, they could feel the weight of history, the secrets that had been concealed within these walls. The room was lavishly decorated, a contrast to the secrets it held. Chandeliers glittered above, casting a surreal glow over the scene.

They began their search, combing through documents, uncovering connections, finding evidence of The Midnight Order's true agenda. The pieces fell into place, the puzzle coming together.

The Midnight Order was not just hiding the nature of the veil; they were orchestrating a network of influence and manipulation that reached far and wide. The extent of their power was breathtaking, the implications staggering.

As they delved deeper, they realised that they had only scratched the surface. The Midnight Order's reach extended to places they had never imagined, its grasp tightening around the very fabric of society.

They had found what they were looking for, but the fight was far from over.

With the evidence in hand, they retreated, knowing that the real battle lay ahead. They had uncovered the secrets, exposed the lies, but the challenge of exposing The Midnight Order to the public remained.

They left Flinders Street Station with a sense of accomplishment but also a sense of foreboding. The Midnight Order was powerful, cunning, relentless.

But they were determined, united, unbreakable.

They had faced The Midnight Order in their hidden headquarters and emerged victorious.

But the war was not over.

CHAPTER 7.6: STALKED IN THE SHADOWS

In the weeks that followed, the pressure from The Midnight Order became nearly unbearable. The trio was no longer just chasing after secrets—they were being hunted. The distinct hum of engine sounds around corners, unusual chatter on public transport, and whispered conversations in cafes became common occurrences. They weren't paranoid; they knew they were being followed. Georgia noticed the same black sedan tailing them more than once, its tinted windows ensuring she couldn't make out the driver.

It was one thing to expose an age-old conspiracy; it was another entirely to feel the weight of its pushback daily. They were up against an organisation. with resources, connections, and a vested interest in ensuring their agenda remained concealed.

But while The Midnight Order posed a direct and apparent threat, the public's response was a different beast. As news of their discoveries started filtering into mainstream media, skeptics and cynics emerged from the woodwork. Talk shows brought in 'experts' who dismissed the veil's significance, dubbing it a mere art piece or a misunderstood artefact. Journalists questioned their credentials, conspiracy theorists spun wilder tales that overshadowed their factual findings, and the masses grew confused and divided.

Heidi, who had been their public face, now faced backlash. The trio watched as, overnight, she went from being an enthusiastic historian to being labelled a sensationalist, with motives being questioned and credibility ridiculed. "The public's a fickle creature," Georgia remarked one evening, scrolling through an online article that discredited Heidi's past work. "One moment you're their champion, the next you're a pariah."

Yet, it was Tim's internal battle that added another layer of complexity to their quest. He often found himself caught in introspection, gazing blankly at a wall in deep thought of the veil's intricate patterns as if seeking answers. Georgia and Heidi would find him sometimes, lost in thought, his eyes filled with a mix of determination and dread.

One evening, Georgia found him on the balcony of his Mernda townhouse, the city's glow onto the overhead night clouds painting a backdrop. "It's all so overwhelming," Tim whispered, avoiding eye contact. "I just... What if this is bigger than us? What if this isn't our fight?"

Georgia stepped closer, placing a comforting hand on his shoulder. "Tim, this is precisely our fight. We might not have chosen it, but it chose us. We can't back down now. Not when we're this close."

He looked at her, the weight of the world seemingly pressing on him. "But at what cost, Georgia? We're risking our lives, our reputations. For what?"

"For the truth," she responded, a fierce determination in her voice. "For all those who've been kept in the dark for so long. We owe it to them. To ourselves. To Noah."

He sighed, leaning into the railing, the city's distant lights flickering like distant stars. "It's just that, sometimes, I wonder if we're ready for the truth. If the world is."

Georgia stood by him, sharing the heavy silence. She too felt the enormity of their mission, the weight of the expectations. But unlike Tim, she was more resolute, more unwavering. The journey had made her stronger, more determined.

"We'll find a way," she finally said, breaking the stillness. "Together."

CHAPTER 7.7: RISKING EVERYTHING

As time went on, they came to realise the full extent of what they were risking. The truth had become a luxury they were paying for with every strained relationship, every ounce of mental and physical strength, and each piece of their normal lives they left behind. The suspense was no longer a thrilling backdrop but a thick fog of uncertainty that clouded their every move.

Yet, in the face of all this, the trio continued their quest. They pressed forward despite the odds, guided by the belief that the truth was within their grasp. Georgia became their pillar, her resilience and relentless determination driving them forward when all seemed lost. Heidi, though bearing the brunt of public criticism, displayed an unwavering commitment to their cause, working tirelessly to piece together evidence and make sense of the intricate web of deception The Midnight Order had woven over centuries.

The threat to their safety was constant. Every move they made was watched, every meeting potentially compromised. They were forced to communicate through codes and subtle messages, leaving nothing to chance. While the possibility of physical danger had been a distant thought before, it now became a chilling reality they had to contend with daily. Nevertheless, they knew they had to push on, for the risk of staying silent was even greater.

Tim's struggle, however, was a battle of a different kind. His fear wasn't of physical harm or public ridicule, but of the unknown. The more he learned about the veil and its significance, the more he feared the implications. The prospect of an age-old truth concealed and manipulated for centuries was not just daunting—it was terrifying.

Yet, as the day of their final confrontation with The Midnight Order drew closer, Tim found himself wrestling with these fears and emerging stronger. He realised that he could no longer afford to wallow in self-doubt. The burden of the truth was indeed heavy, but he was not bearing it alone. He had Georgia and Heidi by his side, sharing the load, shouldering the risk, and fighting the same battle. It was this realisation that finally drove away his fears.

"I'm not afraid," he declared one day, standing in front of Georgia and Heidi, his voice resonating with newfound resolve. "I've been afraid of what this all means, of what we might uncover. But not anymore. We're in this together. And together, we'll face whatever comes our way."

And so, they continued, fuelled by their shared determination. As they navigated the perilous path towards truth, they could sense the climax of their quest drawing near. It was a moment of truth that they had been working towards relentlessly, and it was almost within their grasp. The suspense was high, the risks even higher, but the trio was resolute, ready to confront whatever lay ahead.

In the heart of the bustling city, within the majestic halls of Flinders Street Station, they prepared for the final battle. The truth was within reach. It was time to expose it to the world.

CHAPTER 7.8: VEIL'S AWAKENING

The cool night air buzzed with the anticipation of the imminent confrontation as the trio found themselves before the grandeur of Flinders Street Station. The light of the full moon bathed the historical structure in an ethereal glow. It was silent, a stark contrast to the tumult that Tim, Georgia, and Heidi were feeling internally.

With a grim determination, they passed under the clocks of the famous entrance on the corner of Flinders Street. The vaulted ceilings echoed their footfalls as they made their way towards the upper ballroom – the secret headquarters of The Midnight Order.

Tim felt an odd sense of calm descending on him as they journeyed deeper into the belly of the beast. He could feel the pulsing energy of the veil, its call resonating stronger with each step. It was like a magnet, drawing him in with a power he'd never known before. This was not fear, not anxiety, but a profound connection that he was only now beginning to understand.

The veil was calling to him, the echoes of its timeless whispers guiding him. As they reached the door to the ballroom, he could feel its presence on the other side. He could sense the members of The Midnight Order, waiting in anticipation, unaware of the revelations that were about to unfold. This was no longer just about exposing a secret society; it was about shattering the understanding of reality as they knew it.

The door to the ballroom opened onto a scene that was almost surreal. Members of The Midnight Order, dressed in ceremonial garb, stood in a perfect circle around the present veil. The veil itself seemed to pulsate, its shimmering surface reflecting the soft glow from the chandeliers above.

The members turned at their entrance, surprise evident on their faces. Any formality they were expecting was shattered as the trio stepped into the room, their determined faces telling a story of resilience and fortitude.

"Stop!" Tim's voice echoed through the room, halting the proceedings. He stepped forward, his gaze unflinching as he stared down the members of the order. There was a moment of stunned silence as the members took in the audacity of the intrusion.

"I've come to claim what's rightfully mine," Tim stated, his voice resonating with a conviction that belied his outward appearance. The connection he felt with the veil was stronger than ever, and he could feel its call, its urgency to be free from the clutches of the clandestine organisation.

A hush fell over the room as Tim moved towards the veil, his every step echoing the resolve that had brought them this far. The Order members looked on, a mixture of disbelief and alarm on their faces. This was not a scenario they had anticipated. Their secrecy had always been their most potent weapon, but now it was being challenged in the most profound manner.

Tim stood before the veil, his eyes filled with an understanding that had eluded him till now. The veil seemed to react to his presence, its surface rippling, reaching out to him. He stretched his hand towards it, feeling a jolt of energy pass through him as his fingertips brushed against it. It was like a shock of electricity, a current that seared through his body, jolting his very essence.

In that moment, he was not just Tim, the seeker of truth. He was a part of something far greater, far more profound. The veil was a part of him, and he was a part of it. This revelation, this understanding, gave him a sense of power, a clarity that had been missing before. It was as if he was seeing the world through a new lens, one that peeled back the layers of reality to reveal the extraordinary that lay beneath the ordinary.

He pulled back, his gaze never leaving the veil. The room was silent as everyone watched, their breaths held, their bodies tense. Tim turned to face them, his expression resolute. "The truth will come out," he declared, his voice echoing with a certainty that sent shivers down the spines of The Midnight Order members. "Your time of operating in shadows is over."

He was met with wide eyes, faces pale in the dim light. They didn't know how to respond, their world of secrecy and power disrupted in an instant. Tim, Georgia, and Heidi stood together, the gravity of their journey weighing heavily on them. But with Tim's newfound connection to the veil and the realisation that accompanied it, they knew they were ready for whatever came next.

They had taken the first step in shattering the understanding of reality as they knew it, and there was no turning back now.

The confrontation with The Midnight Order was here. It was now.

CHAPTER 7.9: THE FINAL BATTLE

Before the colossal crystal chandelier stood the figure of the Chairman, his frosty demeanour a stark contrast to the intensity building within the room. Tim felt a surge of confidence, the intimate connection he'd developed with the veil radiating strength through him. He glanced at Georgia and Heidi, their faces glowing with determination.

Tim cleared his throat, his voice reverberating through the vast hall. "For too long," he began, "the true nature of the veil and its connection with us has been concealed, twisted to serve the narrow interests of a few." He turned his gaze towards the Chairman. "Today, that changes."

Every eye in the room was on Tim. The tension was palpable as he continued, revealing the secrets that had been shrouded for generations. The Chairman's confident smirk wavered as Tim shed light on the veil's true purpose and the potential of its powers. The other members of The Midnight Order listened, their faces draining of colour as the reality of their actions sank in.

The enormity of the deception that had been unveiled sent shockwaves through the room. Yet, in the face of the revealed truth, Tim stood tall, his voice not faltering once as he laid bare the foundation of their misguided belief system.

Their audience had swelled beyond the grand room. Unbeknown to the Chairman, Georgia had initiated a live stream, broadcasting their confrontation to the public. Their secrets were being laid bare for the world to see. The veil was being lifted, both figuratively and literally.

As Tim continued to speak, the expressions of the members of The Midnight Order turned from shock to denial and finally to desperation. Yet, there was no escaping the truth. The very foundation on which their Order had been built was crumbling, and with it, the false sense of superiority they had held for so long.

Georgia, her hands steady on the camera, panned to capture the room's atmosphere. The world was watching the downfall of The Midnight Order. The tension in the room was infectious, reaching out to those on the other side of the screen.

As Tim delivered his final sentence, a heavy silence descended on the room. The Chairman stood rigid, his piercing gaze stuck to Tim. The audience, on both sides of the screen, held their collective breath. Then, a wave of chaos swept through the grand ballroom. Shouts filled the room as some members rose in defiance, while others bowed their heads in shame.

However, in the face of the tumult, the trio stood undeterred. Their victory was not marked by cheers and celebration. Instead, it was the sobering reality of the unveiled secrets and the weight of the lies exposed. Yet, there was a sense of relief, a quiet satisfaction that resonated among them. Their struggle was not in vain.

Suddenly, the roaring chaos of the room was punctuated by a burst of laughter. All eyes turned to Georgia, her radiant smile cutting through the tension.

"Well," she said, her laughter subsiding into a wide grin, "I think we've earned ourselves a new title. How about 'the Tricky Trio'?" The lighthearted remark, contrasted against the tense backdrop, struck a chord, and Heidi couldn't help but chuckle. Even Tim managed a small smile.

Yes, the battle had been tough, the journey exhausting, and their victory, bittersweet. But as they stood together in the middle of the grand ballroom, they felt a sense of closure. They had uncovered the truth, stood up against a formidable adversary, and had emerged stronger.

The aftermath of the confrontation would be far-reaching. The world now knew about The Midnight Order, the veil, and the lengths to which some would go to harness its powers. The trio had changed the course of their world, a hefty realisation that would linger with them. Yet, for that moment, amidst the turmoil they had triggered, they found a sense of accomplishment.

Their smiles mirrored the dawn of a new era. A sense of closure lingered in the air, wrapping up this phase of their lives. However, there was also anticipation for what was to come, a promise of a new beginning waiting for them.

CHAPTER 8.1: ECHOES OF VICTORY

In the stillness of dawn, the silhouette of Flinders Street Station appeared to the trio more like a fallen fortress than an ancient transportation hub landmark. Its walls, a canvas for countless stories, now bore the indelible mark of the night's revelatory struggle. Not a word was spoken as Tim, Georgia, and Heidi sat upstairs at Transport Hotel Bar opposite the station, overlooking the monument of their victory. As the first rays of the sun began to trickle over the cityscape, casting the grandeur of the historic structure into sharp relief, they found themselves at the crossroads of triumph and trepidation. 7News, one of the city's major news outlets, had been swift to pick up the story, their shocking exposé painting the headlines with bold declarations of the truth about the veil and the downfall of The Midnight Order. The world was waking up to a new reality, and the response was as diverse as the people themselves.

Ripples of this paradigm-shifting story had begun to infiltrate the heart of Melbourne. Social media channels were ablaze with debates, theories, and disbelief. Some dismissed it as an elaborate hoax, others celebrated the revelation as liberation from the mundane. Yet, there were those who reacted with fear and confusion, unable to reconcile this new reality with their existing world views. Each comment, social media post, or article further fuelled the growing whirlpool of public opinion.

The trio sat together, each lost in their thoughts, each grappling with the weight of the change they'd instigated. Despite their valiant victory, their hearts bore the burden of uncertainty.

"You know," Georgia began, her gaze still locked onto the station opposite, "I never thought I'd see the day when our crazy adventure would make front-page news." A bitter-sweet smile played on her lips, reflecting the tumultuous cocktail of emotions swirling within her. She turned her phone screen towards Tim and Heidi, displaying an article titled, 'The Veil: An Intricate Tapestry of Reality or a Fringe Conspiracy Theory?'

Tim took a deep breath, his fingers absentmindedly tapping on the table. The veil was real; there was no denying it now. But what would the world do with this reality? Would they dismiss it, fear it, or embrace it? "We've opened Pandora's box, haven't we?" he murmured, his voice barely audible over the hum of the waking city.

Heidi looked at her companions, her countenance radiating a calm determination. "We've opened their eyes, yes. But maybe that's what the world needed. A jolt out of their comfort zones. It's not our place to determine how they should react or what they should believe. We've played our part; the rest is up to them."

"Spoken like a true journalist," Georgia chuckled lightly, easing the tense atmosphere.

"We might have stirred up a storm, but at least it's a storm of thought, of questioning," Tim added, his expression thoughtful. "We've given them a chance to see beyond their usual horizon. It's up to them what they do with that."

Their resolve was firm, yet the seeds of doubt were hard to ignore. The reality of the veil, the mysterious energy field interwoven with the fabric of existence, had been a startling revelation for them too. Now, they were at the helm of a journey that had the potential to change the way humanity perceived their existence. The 'Tricky Trio,' as Georgia liked to call them, had indeed played their part.

The question that lingered was, what would the world do with the truth now laid bare?